DOOMSDAY

An Edward Mendez, P. I. Thriller

Book 9

Gerard Denza

Doomsday
An Edward Mendez, P. I. Thriller
Book IX

This novel is entirely a work of fiction. The names, characters, and incidents portrayed in it are the work of the author's imagination. Any resemblance to actual persons, living or dead, events or locations, is entirely coincidental.

Copyright 2023 Gerard Denza

All rights reserved ISBN: 979-8-8580539-4-1

No part of this publication may be reproduced stored in or introduced into a retrieval system, or transmitted in any form, or by any means, without written permission of the copyright owner.

Cover art: Book Covers Art

Also available digitally.

BY THE SAME AUTHOR:

Icarus: The Collected Plays

Ramsay: Dealer of Death

The Time Deceiver:
An Edward Mendez, P. I. Thriller, Book I

Night Drifter:
An Edward Mendez, P. I. Thriller, Book II

The Immortal:
An Edward Mendez, P. I. Thriller, Book III

Target: The Bogeyman:
An Edward Mendez, P. I. Thriller, Book IV

The Deadliest Game:
An Edward Mendez, P. I. Thriller, Book V

Romo-Ark:
An Edward Mendez, P. I. Thriller, Book VI

Disappearance:
An Edward Mendez, P. I. Thriller, Book VII

The Angel:
An Edward Mendez, P. I. Thriller, Book VIII

Cast of Characters:

Edward Mendez – a private investigator who must turn assassin to save the world.
Yolanda Estravades – Edward's girlfriend who has some disturbing news for the P. I.
Dottie Mendez – Edward Mendez's personal assistant and sister.
Lt. William Donovan – a police Lieutenant who must turn assassin to save the world.
Marco Morales – a Police Officer at the 86th Precinct who is a friend of Edward Mendez.
Nathalie Montaigne – a woman with a sordid past who has somehow managed to escape criminal prosecution.
Werner Hoffman – an associate of Miss Montaigne who has his eye on a priceless artifact.
Lorraine Keyes – a familiar face from the past who is destined to affect Edward Mendez's life.
Irene Wong – a brilliant scientist who accompanies Edward Mendez on his trip to the recent past.
Marlena Lake – a woman who is versed in the occult and has connections in the underworld.
Mabel Scott – proud landlady of a Sullivan St. apartment building.
Nathan Zhou – an aspiring young actor who is not above taking a bribe.
Bao Liu – an aspiring young actor who knows a lot more than he's telling.
Walter – an aspiring young actor who is not above taking a bribe and lying to a police official.

Morgan Andes – a Police Officer at the 86th Precinct and good friend of Edward Mendez.

Tracy Thielen – a businesswoman and girlfriend of Morgan Andes.

Nella Mendez – Edward Mendez's youngest sister who may have knowledge of the end of the world.

Mrs. Isabelle Mendez – Edward Mendez's strong willed mother.

Victoria Mendez – Edward Mendez's beautiful sister.

Ginny Gray – ace reporter who may be on to the story of her career.

Susan Broder – an intelligent woman who is her mother's "right-hand-man."

Manuel Mendez – Edward Mendez's father who sends his son on a trip to the past to save mankind.

Roger Lee – a gangster who operates out of New York City's Chinatown. He is cunning and dangerous.

Detective Hopper – of the 6th Precinct in Brooklyn. He's been assigned to the Lorraine Keyes case.

Jamie Anne Farley – a young woman who works at the Information Desk in a Manhattan skyscraper.

Romeo Duquesne – a young teenager who has a *very* vivid dream.

Karl Fassbinder – a Nazi engineer.

Lisa Pabst – a Nazi scientist.

Heinrich Weiss – a Nazi engineer.

Alexandra Raymond – works out of the 86th Precinct.

Table of Contents

Part I Chance Meeting?..1

Part II Miss Lorraine Keyes 70

Part III Doomsday...112

Part IV The Assassins...137

Part V The Deserted City 201

Part I
Chance Meeting?

ONE

IT WAS a Wednesday morning and not a good one. Edward Mendez was taking a long distance phone call from his girlfriend, Yolanda Estravades, who was in Brazil on an ice skating tour. What city? Edward assumed it was Rio de Janiero. He didn't know. He didn't really care, at least not at this point in the conversation.

Edward was sitting at his desk in his third floor office in lower Manhattan. He was staring out the window that looked on to Broadway: traffic was still heavy and people were still hurrying to their jobs. The P. I. didn't notice any of this...not really. His Latin temper was beginning to flare up and he was looking to punch somebody out.

-Hello, Edward? Are you still there? Please, answer me. Try not to be too angry with me. Please.

-I'm still here. The initial blast is over. So you found yourself a rich Brazilian: a coffee plantation magnate. What's he worth, baby?

-Don't talk like that as if I'm some sort of gold-digger.

-I'll talk any way I damned well please. What's his name? Give me a name so I can spit at it.

-Why do you want to know? What difference can it make to you?

-I'm a private dick. I like to know things. Give.

-No. I won't tell you.

-Why, Yolanda? Afraid I'll do some checking up on him...find out a few things...like a sordid past...s couple of skeletons in the boy's closet?

Edward couldn't keep the sarcasm out of his voice. He didn't want to. He wanted to hurt her like she was hurting him.

-I want a husband. Is that so very wrong?

-A rich husband.

-And children.

Now, Edward was incredulous.

-Since when? I know the answer to that question: to any man with enough money.

-You're being mean. I want stability in my life. Edward, I still love you, but I'm afraid of the dark world that surrounds you.

Doomsday

-You're part of it. You've always been a part of it. And, what makes you think you can separate yourself from it...and me? I've tried. It doesn't leave you alone, Yolanda. Take my word for it. Accept your fate and make the best of it.

-Maybe, I know that. But, I must try.

-Is he a good man?

-Yes. I think so.

-Handsome?

-Yes. But, not as handsome as you. It doesn't matter.

-When is the holy event to take place?

-In October at his parents' house, in Rio.

-Am I invited?

-Do you want to come?

-No.

-I understand.

-Well, baby, this call's costing you a bundle, but I guess your new boyfriend can afford it. I'll say goodbye...and that's a final goodbye. It's finished with us. Savvy?

He didn't wait for an answer. He started noticing the traffic outside. His neck muscles started easing up. His breathing became regular. He started to reach for a cigarette and wishing that he could blow the smoke in her face.

-Edward?

-Goodbye, Yolanda.

The P. I. hung up the phone. He got up and leaned out the window to take in some fresh air. The cool breeze felt good. It was a northerly wind and quite bracing and for a short while, he let himself be cooled off.

When he'd had enough of the morning breeze, he pulled himself back inside. Now, what? That was easy. He had cases to look into and a few loose threads to tie up. He adjusted his tie and sat back down at his desk. He took out a Lucky Strike and lit up.

After a few deep drags, he reached for the manila folder that was marked: Susan Broder. He flipped through the dozen or so pages and stopped at the last one: a verbatim transcript of the phone conversations between Marlena Lake and Roger Lee as taken down by Alexandra Raymond. A ransom of $500,000 had been paid and lost...lost to Mr. Roger Lee. Why in God's name had Lt. Donovan done it? Crazy, stupid bastard. They could have stuffed Monopoly money in that briefcase. Susan Broder had been saved and hollow threats oughta' be laughed at. Why didn't Donovan laugh? Had he gone soft or something? Was he trying to prove something that no one else could figure out?

Edward shook his head. He really didn't care...well, not that much anyway. This little debacle was Donovan's headache, not his. He'd been against paying Roger Lee one red cent.

Doomsday

But, it wasn't this that Edward was looking into. It was the dialogue between Marlena and Roger Lee. He read through the transcript, again. How did Roger Lee know about his father, Manuel Mendez? How did Roger Lee know that Miranda Drake had any kind of wealth? Well, that last one was easy. Miss Drake's hospital records were easily accessible but...that part about Manuel Mendez bleeding his benefactress... Roger Lee knew a lot more that he should have known.

Edward put the file back into the file cabinet and made ready to leave. He put on his tan blazer and adjusted his white open collar shirt. He took out his paperback book, 1984, and tossed it on to his desk. He wasn't in the mood for reading...not now, anyway. He stepped out into the reception area.

-Hey, Dottie? I didn't have any breakfast. I'm gonna' head on out for a bite to eat. You know the place, Sam's Bar n' Grill. Hold down the fort.

Dottie Mendez saw the distraught look on her brother's face. She had overhead part of the conversation and she was just as upset.

-Eddie? Are you okay? You look a little frazzled. Did that long distance call upset you?

-Yes. My girlfriend handed me a "Dear John" via long distance. In other words, she dumped me. See you later.

Lt. William Donovan had just come off a real bad night to an even worse Wednesday morning. Quite conceivably, he could be kicked off the Police Force...or worse, demoted to desk duty or Patrol Officer status. Take your pick.

In God's name why? *Why*? He couldn't answer that question...not honestly, at least not until his emotions had cooled down. A half-a-million down the friggin' drain. Still no word of outrage from either Marlena Lake or Manuel Mendez...and that was damned strange. It did help Lt. Donovan keep some professional focus, though. But, it didn't let him off the hook, not by a long shot.

Roger Lee had been too clever. He had money and resources and cunning and- Hold on. Where did that thug's money come from ? Lt. Donovan had gotten the distinct impression that Roger Lee had been hard up for cash and that he'd been operating on a "shoe-string"...on fake credit and promises. Something just didn't add up here. The man had been heavily in debt to various loan sharks. His credit was as rotten as his morals.

Lt. Donovan reached for his phone and called in Marco Morales. Officer Morales had been expecting this phone call and was prepared. He walked right in without knocking. He liked the Lieutenant's office which was compact and neat and organized.

-Marco? You waiting outside the door?

-You bet.

-Good. We got a lot of homework to go over before they kick me off of the damned Force.

Office Morales laughed, but not too hard. He was as worried as his superior was.

-That's not gonna' happen. I was doing field work this week and came up with three leads who wanna' talk their heads off.

Lt. Donovan leaned forward eagerly in his chair. Good news...he tried not to get too excited.

-Three canaries?

-You bet. And, they're in the Interrogation Room now just waiting to "sing." They're scared and just might want to cut a deal.

-Then, what the hell are we waiting for? Let's go. Time's not on my side.

Marco got up, scraping the wooden chair on the floor. Lt. Donovan opened the door for them.

-You first, Officer.

Nathalie Montaigne had made a full recovery from her "dirty" needle attack. It had taken months to recover from her ordeal at the hands of that filthy priest, but with the help of her good friends, Werner Hoffman and Grace Stone, she had succeeded in regaining not only her health, but in securing an honest livelihood. She and Mr. Hoffman had gone into business together. They operated and owned the occult bookshop on 18th

St. on Manhattan's West Side. It was situated in the middle of the block on the north side with a colorful banner affixed to a flagpole outside the building waving in the breeze..

After months of preparation, the bookshop was cleaned of all debris and its bookcases were now lined with new editions of various occult literature: books that were either out of print or difficult to get. The finances for this venture had been supplied by Werner Hoffman. He was the silent partner while Nathalie took care of business "up front."

Their clientele consisted of residents from the East and West Villages of Manhattan, but customers also came in from the outer boroughs and even New Jersey. Most of their customers lived on the "edge" of society. People who did not fit into the mainstream of life: the outcasts, the aesthetes, the avaunt-garde.

Nathalie was standing behind the front counter at this moment talking to her "silent" partner.

-Business, dear Werner, is good, but not exceptional.

-I can see that from the ledgers. But, it takes time to establish a business such as ours. What do you suggest?

-We must include the classics in our stock. That would attract the university trade and the more pedestrian customer.

Werner Hoffman smiled at his partner's suggestion and took a drag on his cigarette.

-Ah, yes! Shakespeare, Marlowe, Collins. It might work. We'll have to contact their respective publishers.

-And, the modern classics, as well.

-Such as, my dear? I didn't know that there were any.

-Fitzgerald, Rand, Faulkner. And, more that I cannot at present think of. We should start today and display those book in our shop window.

-I'll go upstairs and get started. Shouldn't be too hard. We'll take them on consignment. This bookshop does have a reputation of sorts from the previous owners. You take care of any customers that might come in and let them know what we're planning. Keep our guest "log" on the counter.

-Of course. Repeat customers are always welcome.

Nathalie picked up the newspaper that was lying on the counter. A story...an article...on the front page caught her eye. She pointed it out to her partner.

-Take a look at this, would you? A half million dollars gone. It's about the Susan Broder kidnapping. The girl was rescued, it seems, but the ransom money and the surviving kidnapper are still missing.

-What of it, my dear?

-Edward Mendez is involved in this case. And, that is a man who is always of interest to me.

-A man of many talents.

Werner Hoffman took another drag on his cigarette and then put it out in the glass ashtray on the counter.

-I better go on up and get started on those calls.

-Yes. Of course.

Werner Hoffman walked to the back of the store where a spiral staircase led to Nathalie's apartment. He climbed the metal stairwell and let himself into the apartment.

Meanwhile, Nathalie was still reading the article when a customer walked in. It was Nella Mendez.

TWO

EDWARD MENDEZ walked into Sam's Bar n' Grill which was just off of Broadway and Hector St. It was a small place that gave you a choice of sitting in a booth or at a side table near the back. The P.I. chose the side table and ordered a grilled cheese sandwich and a whiskey and soda. It was early in the day for liquor, but this was a special occasion...an occasion for smoldering and resentment.

The whiskey and soda came first. When the waiter put it down, he leaned over and said a few words to the P. I.

-Shouldn't be serving liquor so early in the day, but you're a regular and I know you. Had a bad day, man? I can tell.

-In one simple word: yes. I should've ordered a double.

-Finish that one first and see how you feel. Things might look a little better.

-I'll settle for less worse.

-It's still early in the day, man. Buck up! We're in a city that's full of possibilities.

The waiter moved off and Edward took a long sip of his drink. Oh, yeah... It went down easy...not the best Scotch on the planet, but it would do just fine for now. He stretched out his legs, sat back and tried to relax, still holding on to his drink. Was he the only customer in the place? Looked like it. The waiter was standing at the bar and having a drink of water...or vodka

Edward's back was to the door when he heard it open.

-I guess I've got company.

It was a young woman. He could smell the scent of her perfume and hear the click of her high heels.

-Stiletto heels, I bet.

And, the fragrance...nice but not too expensive. It was sort of like the scent of misty air after a thunder storm.

Edward fought the temptation to turn around and look. He really wasn't in the mood for company. The young woman saved him the trouble.

-Hello. Would you mind some company? I'd like to order a drink and I hate drinking alone. Doesn't give a respectable appearance

Edward got up in spite of himself. He never refused a pretty girl anything if he could help it.

-Sure. Have a seat.

-Thanks. You're a sport.

The girl sat down and Edward recognized her at once.

-You're the girl on the subway train.

-And, you're the boy who didn't make a pass. That wasn't very nice.

Edward signaled the waiter over.

-I had a lot on my plate that day, but I did notice you.

-I know you did.

-And, I remembered you.

-Name's Lorraine Keyes. I'm a freelance interior decorator who's still learning her trade, Mr. Private Investigator.

The waiter came over to their table.

-Lorraine? What'll you have?

-Gin and tonic and heavy on the ice.

The waiter took the order and left.

-Lorraine? You've got one helluva' great smile.

Miss Keyes crossed her lovely legs and slipped off her sweater.

-There. It keeps that damned chill out. And- Edward? Are you okay? I think your mind just drifted out of your gorgeous body.

The P. I. shook himself.

-Was it something I said? I'm not the sensitive type. You can level with me.

-It *was* something you said, baby.

-Like what? I don't usually have that effect on men.

-Like that persistent damned chill in the air! It practically never goes away.

He downed the rest of his drink just as the waiter brought over Lorraine's.

-Thanks.

-Refill for me.

-Sure thing, pal.

-Edward?

-Yes?

-Eat your grilled cheese sandwich before it gets cold.

The P. I. took a bite out of it without really tasting it.

-Now, maybe, I shouldn't ask this, but where's your ice skating girlfriend? Personally, I wouldn't let you out of my sight.

Still holding on to the grilled cheese sandwich.

-She dumped me for a coffee bean jockey.

-You're kidding?

-No. Lorraine? Do you live in the city?

-Down on Sullivan St. It's just a stone's throw from West 4th St.. You know, where the Bohemian set hangs out.

-I've got some time to kill, baby. How about inviting me on up? You live on your own?

-I do. Or should I pretend to have a roommate?

The waiter brought over Edward's drink.

-Thanks, pal.

The waiter gave Edward a knowing smile and sauntered on back to the bar.

-Hey, Lorraine, a toast to a real pleasant morning that sure didn't start out that way.

Lorraine Keyes smiled showing perfect white teeth.

-I'll drink to that. And, thanks for the compliment.

-You want some of this sandwich? It's not half bad.

-Yes, Edward. I'd love a bite.

Irene Wong was in her second floor apartment on Eighth St. It was a one bedroom flat with a fully equipped bathroom and kitchen. The Asian scientist liked the place because she had decorated it to be cozy, neat and functional. The living room where she was now sitting was painted a pastel brown and all the furniture and rugs and curtains matched in varying shades of that color. The bedroom was a soft pink and the kitchen an egg shell white. The bathroom was milk white to match the porcelain fixtures. It was a lovely place and what a shame that her lease was about to run out.

Irene was working at her desk, trying to balance equations that would not balance...attempting to plot a trajectory that would not fall into place.

-But, it must or else there is no hope for any of us.

She re-wrote the equations on a fresh sheet of paper.

-Perhaps, if I had access to Dr. Lange's notes, it would help. It must help! I wish he were here with me now.

Her hands began to shake. She put down the pencil and got up from the desk. The problem was that she couldn't focus entirely on her work. How could she when faced with possible deportation? She wanted to scream and tear her notes into little pieces.

She paced the small living room and decided upon a course of action.

-I must contact Dr. Lange's office. They must allow me access to his notes.

She sat down, again, got out her address book, and dialed Dr. Lange's old office. No answer.

-Perhaps, it's been shut down due to Dr. Moreland's recent death? But, Mary Riley would still be there. I must keep trying.

And, then, Irene had another idea.

-That woman, Marlena Lake…I liked her and she offered me help and even a safe asylum. I'll call her. I've nothing to lose.

She flipped through her address book. She dialed Marlena's number. The phone was picked up on the second ring.

-Hello? Who is this?

-Miss Lake? It's Irene Wong. I'll get straight to the point. I need your help.

Doomsday

-Come right over, my dear. I'll prepare some tea. And, what is it you need? It sounds rather urgent.

-It is most urgent. It involves Dr. Lange and the sun's disappearance in 1947.

-Come by cab. I will pay the fare. And, hurry, my dear.

-Mr. Edward Mendez, if you're looking for a new girlfriend, let me be the first to apply for the position. And, I'm not joking.

Edward had just pulled out and was now lying naked next to the very pretty Lorraine Keyes. He reached over and stroked that soft, wet spot. But, then, he looked at his wristwatch...the one that Yolanda had given him for a birthday present. It was late morning and he had things to do. He didn't want to leave this beautiful girl, but his erection was subsiding and if he kept this close to the girl, his rod would be headed uptown, again.

He forced himself to sit up and get dressed.

-Gotta' go, baby.

-As a matter of fact, so do I. Kiss goodbye, until the next time?

He bent over and kissed her hard on the mouth. She tried to draw him back to her, but he resisted.

-Baby, save it for the next time. This private dick's gotta' head uptown and my car's still in the repair shop.

She pretended to be hurt.

-I can take a hint. The subway is just two blocks up. It'll take you straight uptown.

Edward was pulling on his pants. Lorraine was just what he needed, but the time had to be made up. He was sitting on the edge of the bed and putting on his socks. He looked over his shoulder at Lorraine who was getting into her slip.

-Hey, baby, I'm all out of cigarettes. Got one?
-Sure.

She reached over and opened a drawer on the end table next to the bed.

-Help yourself.

She handed Edward the pack of cigarettes.

-Hey, Lucky Strike. My brand. That's a good sign, baby, that we're compatible.

He bent over to lace up his shoes.

-Okay, that just about does it.

He got up and grabbed his jacket off of the armchair. Lorraine came over to him.

-I'll walk you to the door and I'll even wave goodbye.

-Then, let's go.

Edward opened the door, waved goodbye and climbed down the stairs. Lorraine lived on the second floor of a three story apartment building. Halfway down the stairs, Edward realized that he still had her pack of Lucky Strike on him.

-Hey, baby? Catch.

He threw the half empty pack up to her and she caught it with cupped hands. Edward turned around and noticed a middle-aged woman standing in the foyer's doorway. She was smiling at Edward. Lorraine, catching sight of her, waved hello.

-Hi, Mrs. Scott!

-Hello, dear.

Edward smiled and tipped his hat to the woman.

-Nice meeting you.

-Have a nice day, young man.

And, with a Cheshire smile on his face...

-I'm Lorraine's new boyfriend, but don't tell her that.

Edward opened the outside door and stepped out on to the stoop. He took a drag on his cigarette and climbed down the stairs. He walked toward the subway station, not seeing the silhouette of a man standing across the street from Lorraine's building...a man who now crossed the street and entered Lorraine Keyes's apartment building.

THREE

-HEY, BILL? I almost forgot: this envelope came for you. Alex handed it to me just a few minutes ago.

-Where is Miss Raymond?

-Over at Marlena Lake's place tying up some loose ends, I guess.

-Like a quarter of a million of them?

Lt. Donovan was secretly pleased to hear this. He had wanted to infiltrate Miss Lake's inner circle for some time. Good. Alex hadn't forgotten his "personal" assignment for her. The Dolores Sarney case was still open along with the Lieutenant's animosity toward Edward Mendez and Marlena Lake. .

-One second, Marco. Let me just look at this first.

Lt. Donovan carefully opened the sealed envelope. As a trained police officer, you never took chances with any correspondence. The flap of the envelope came open. He took out the folded paper which felt strange...didn't feel like standard paper.

He unfolded it and read:

"Just before dawn of the 27th of May, you and Edward Mendez must turn back the clock. Go to the top of Manhattan's Flatiron Building and do as you are told."

The print on the paper looked similar to that of a teletype print-out, but it wasn't that. And, it wasn't from a standard typewriter.

Lt. Donovan folded it and put it back in the envelope. He shoved it into his back pocket without thinking.

The Lieutenant and Officer Morales entered the Interrogation Room. Seated at the rectangular table were three young men: two Asian and one Caucasian. All three were handsome and similar in appearance: dark, short hair that was neatly combed, clean shaven and thin. All three of them were sporting blazers and a white collared shirt but no tie.

Lt. Donovan addressed them in his professional manner which was not exactly polite, but civil.

-Gentlemen? We'll try not to keep you too long.

He sat down at the head of the table and Officer Morales sat at the opposite end.

-I'll start with you, young man.

The Lieutenant addressed the Asian man seated to his left, but it was the Asian man seated to the Lieutenant's right who responded.

-Excuse me, but my friend speaks practically no English and understands even less.

Lt. Donovan took this in his stride not relying on the veracity of the statement.

-Fair enough. I'll start with you, then. Name?

-Nathan Zhou.

-Where do you live, Nathan?

-In Chinatown on Mott St.. I live with my family.

-Nathan, two days ago, you were spotted at Columbus Circle.

-Yes. I was there. I won't deny it.

-What were you doing there?

Nathan Zhou looked across at his Asian friend. Lt. Donovan caught this and made a mental note of it.

-Look at me and not your friend. Remember? He can't speak English. Does he understand any?

-Very little. I told you that.

-Now, you can answer my question.

-I was with friends and simply passing through. What of it?

-You didn't happen to pick up a valise containing a half million bucks, did you?

-I did not. I would have remembered that.

-Then, I'll let Officer Morales take over. Officer Morales, do you have any questions for Nathan, here?

-A few. Mr. Nathan Zhou. You're an actor.

-Yes. Aspiring.

-You were on a job this past Monday, weren't you?

No response so Lt. Donovan jumped in, this time not bothering to be civil.

Doomsday

-Officer Morales asked you a question. And, if you don't answer, we'll hold you for obstruction.

Nathan Zhou took a deep breath before answering.

-Yes. I was an an extra in a feature film. We were told that, weren't we, Walter.

The Caucasian male nodded and took up the story.

-Nathan's right. We were extras in some kind of feature film on New York City. It was a day's work, that's all.

Officer Morales now addressed "Walter."

-Who approached you and when?

-It was back in March of this year. Can't tell you the exact date.

-Try.

-Toward the beginning of the month, I think.

-And, who was it?

-Who was what?

-Don't play fancy with me, Walter. I'm a simple man. I don't like it.

-I didn't get his name, Officer Morales. Handsome. Tall. Could've been Japanese or Chinese. I don't know. I should, but I don't.

-And, this handsome man paid you up front?

-In cash.

-Trusting that you'd show up? How could he be sure of that?

-Why wouldn't we? Would've been bad for our reputations not to show up. I guess he knew that.

Officer Morales turned his attention back to Lt. Donovan.

-That's it for me. Oh...just one more thing: write down your names, addresses and phone numbers. And, they better be legit.

Lt. Donovan nodded and put out his cigarette. He spoke pointedly to the three young men.

-None of you are to leave town...not for any reason. Got it?

Nathan Zhou and Walter Bain nodded rather solemnly. And, did the third young man begin to nod as well? Lt. Donovan thought that he did.

Officer Morgan Andes and Tracy Thielen were having coffee in her downtown office. The coffee was strong and black with a "biting" taste.

-Good coffee, Tracy. You make this?

-I wish. Came straight from the cafeteria. Glad you like it, though.

Morgan took another sip of his coffee as he took careful note of his attractive girlfriend.

-Tracy?

-Yes, Morgan?

-What's up?

Tracy knew what Morgan meant, but could she tell him? He was a Police Officer and had to adhere to a certain code of ethics and morality. Or was she just plain scared to say anything? It could mean her job which meant a great deal to her. But, it was a secret that should be shared with the right people...people who could conceivably do something about it or at least make an attempt at a solution.

-Morgan, this is difficult for me. It's something that you must not repeat to anyone, at least, not yet.

-Why not?

-It's classified information and it could cause mass panic. Even I shouldn't know about it.

Morgan put down his coffee. He was getting just a little impatient with his girlfriend.

-Tell me. And, make it simple.

-Morgan...the world may be coming to an end slowly but inexorably...or it could even happen tomorrow.

Tracy suppressed a shudder. She felt chilly so she got up and switched off the overhead fan. It didn't help.

Morgan Andes picked up his coffee cup. He held it tightly...almost breaking it.

-How will it happen? When will it happen? And, by the way, Tracy?...this is one secret you had no right to keep to yourself.

Tracy sat back down.

-Morgan, the Earth was knocked off its orbit when the sun did a vanishing act a couple of years back. The gravity that held our world in place was gone and now it's drifting toward interstellar space. At least, that's how Dr. Gerald Lawrence puts it. I don't understand all the scientific jargon.

-But, enough of it that it spells out "doomsday?"

-Yes.

-How the hell does your company know about this?

-We have contacts in Washington and at the Palomar Observatory in California. That's where Dr. Lawrence is based. I met him once. He's a very nice and unassuming man. You'd like him.

Morgan put down his coffee cup. His hand was starting to tremble and he found himself taking deep breaths.

-Hey, Tracy, has Dr. Lawrence come up with a solution? And, that's a "yes" or "no" question.

-He has. But, it's a pretty drastic one and would require international cooperation. Oh, God, Morgan! The solution is even more frightening than the danger itself.

-As my buddy, Eddie Mendez, would say: give.

-It would take a massive atomic detonation to stop the outward drift of the Earth.

-But, would it work?

-Dr. Lawrence thinks that it would, but...

-Keep talking.

-It...the detonation would not only stop the outward drift but it could reverse the drift and hurl the Earth toward the sun.

Doomsday

Tracy had to stop and catch her breath. Morgan almost knocked his coffee cup to the floor. He wanted to smash it.

-I think I understand: freeze to death or be burnt to a cinder.

-Morgan? You may tell this to Eddie Mendez.

-Tracy? Baby? I sure will. He's one helluva' resourceful man.

-And, please tell him today. To hell with my job. He saved us once before, didn't he?

-You bet he did. But, Tracy, these atomic blasts...wouldn't they harm the Earth? And, what about the fall-out?

Tracy suppressed a grin.

-That's why they're putting it off. The so-called "cure" would be even worse than the "disease."

Morgan got to his feet. He wasn't looking at Tracy. He was looking at his coffee cup with overt hatred.

-I'm gonna find Eddie right now. You stay here. I'll be in touch. And, don't lose hope.

Tracy got up and kissed the Police Officer. She held on to him...tightly.

-Oh, Morgan! I'm so glad that I told you!

-Hey, Marco? Follow the silent man. You know, the one who can't speak or understand English? I'll bet!

-Got ya', Lieutenant. He looked plenty scared to me for someone who couldn't understand a word of our lingo.

-Like we were gonna' see through his little masquerade. Follow him, Marco, and put a tail on those other two creeps.

At that moment, Edward Mendez came walking up the stairs. The P. I. greeted the Lieutenant and Officer Morales, who ran past the shamus with a quick hello.

-Where's Marco off to?

-He's tailing a Chinese actor, who I think is part of Roger Lee's gang. Let's step into my office, Mendez.

-You took the words right out of my mouth.

The two men walked across the floor to Lt. Donovan's office.

-Have a seat.

-Cigarette?

-No, thanks. Just had one. Trying to cut back.

-I'm not.

Edward took out a Lucky Strike and lit up.

-I'm glad you showed up, Mendez. We got a lot to talk about.

-Like a half-a-million in ransom money?

-That and this.

Lt. Donovan tossed the white envelope on to his desk.

-Have a look.

Edward took out the note and read it. He, then, put it back in the envelope and tossed it on to the Lieutenant's desk.

-What the hell does it mean?

-I was hoping you could tell me.

-I can't. "...turn back the clock." I don't get it.

-Neither do I. Are you sure that you don't get it, Mendez?

Edward thought about it for a moment.

-Not entirely. There's something in the phrasing that's triggering something off. Can't place it, though.

-What about this script? It's not teletype. It looks like some kind of computer print-out.

-Let me take a look at it, again.

Edward took the note out of the envelope. He turned it upside down and sideways . He even tried reading it from the reverse side.

-I've seen this type of script before.

-Where?

The P. I. took a drag on his cigarette and exhaled the smoke toward the ceiling.

-At Marlena's...in her library.

Lt. Donovan sat back and let out an exaggerated sigh.

-Why am I not surprised. Did she send it? Level with me.

-I don't think so. It's not her style. Confrontation is more in her line. No. This script or..what the hell did she call it...is from one of those books that she and Susan took from that house in Staten Island.

-You mean one of those books from the future...supposedly?

-That just about sums it up. Not sure just what book, but I can check on it easily enough.

-You do that, Mendez. And, let's get back to that half-a-million debacle.

-Any chance of getting any of it back?

-There's always a chance. And, I'm making sure it's a good one.

-Was Marco after one of your leads just now?

The Lieutenant smiled with respect at the P. I..

-You're sharp, Mendez.

-You taking much flack about that ransom money?

-The worst is yet to come. So, I'm trying hard to head it off at the pass.

-Let me know if I can help.

-Check on that note first. Could you do it right now?

-Marlena's townhouse is within walking distance from here and she's usually at home.

-And, get her take on the note's content. She just might have an opinion.

Edward grinned as he got to his feet. He put his cigarette out.

-Marlena Lake *always* has an opinion.

FOUR

-MISS MENDEZ! Such a pleasure to see you once again. How long has it been, cherie? Two years? Perhaps, even more than that, eh? One looses track of time, no? Such a pity that time passes so quickly and mercilessly. But, perhaps you do not recognize me? I have changed and for the worst. One might call me an old hag.

In point of fact, Nella Mendez did not recognize this rather gray and shrunken woman. The voice sounded familiar...the heavy French accent...but it just couldn't be. Could someone age twenty years in just three?

-Time and circumstance have not been kind to Nathalie.

Nathalie Montaigne?

-But, you, cherie, have changed very little.

Nella approached the counter and offered Miss Montaigne her best manners.

-Miss Montaigne. Of course I remember you. The séance at my mother's house. And, Edward has spoken of you.

-Not in ill terms, I trust. He is too much the gentleman for that.

-Yes. He is. Edward did mention that you'd been ill.

-Mon Dieu! That horrid priest pricked me with a dirty needle. I lost quite a bit of weight that I could not afford to lose. I know. I look old and quite shriveled.

-Not at all, Miss Montaigne. You do look thin, but that often happens when one has been ill.

-But, enough about me. What brought you to my humble bookshop?

-You're the new owner? Congratulations and the best of luck. I was afraid the place had closed down.

-I wouldn't hear of it. And, thank you for your good wishes.

Nathalie thought it best not to mention her "silent" partner: Werner Hoffman, at least not yet. Why stir up too many past memories?

-Miss Montaigne, would you have any books on quantum mechanics or the art of time travel?

-Quantum mechanics? I doubt it. But, the subject of time travel...yes we have several books related to the subject. Do you plan on a trip to the future, cherie?

Nella smiled at the Frenchwoman as she took out her compact.

Doomsday

-No. Not to the future, but to the fairly recent past.

-It must be your detective brother who plans on going. How very extraordinary. Come. We must locate those books. And, of course, you must tell me more. I insist that you satisfy my insatiable curiosity..

-Victoria? Please, come here at once. I wish to speak with you.

Victoria Mendez hurried into her mother's bedroom which was on the first floor of the family's Brooklyn brownstone. Isabelle Mendez's bedroom had been recently re-wallpapered in a very pretty lilac background with dainty pink roses throughout. It was a pleasant change from the rather dark, French Renaissance print.

Mrs. Mendez was sitting up in bed when her youngest daughter hurried in.

-Yes, mother? What can I get for you?

-Your company will suffice. And, I will get straight to the point. The journal that your late husband gave you; what is contained in it?

-Mother, what in the world-

-Do not deny it. Remain the honest daughter that you have always been.

-I've never even mentioned my journal to you. How could you possibly know anything about it?

-Catrina told me about it.

Victoria pulled away from her mother's bedside. The young woman was beside herself with anger

-Catrina! I shouldn't be surprised. Even from her grave, she's nothing but a trouble maker.

Mrs. Mendez allowed her daughter to fume for a few moments before she continued her cross examination. But, Victoria wasn't quite finished.

-My rotten sister...prying into my personal effects. How dare she!

-Pity your dead sister. She was murdered.

-I don't! I won't! She got what was coming to her.

-Victoria, control yourself. This outburst does not become you. Catrina would not tell me what your late husband had written in that journal.

-And, why not? You two were such confidantes.

-I don't know. Perhaps, what she read frightened her.

-Good! I hope it gave her sleepless nights. Your late daughter was evil, mother. We all despised her as much as she was contemptuous of us.

-I'm well aware of that. And, now, my dear, what is written in the journal?

-My journal, do you mean? It is *my* journal. Do you hear me, mother? It is not public property.

-I am not deaf. Please, Victoria, may I see your journal and judge its contents for myself? I ask this out of dire need and not mere curiosity.

-Very well, mother. I'll fetch it for you.

Doomsday

Victoria made for the door, but stopped just short of opening it. She glanced back at her mother in bed.

-And, by the way, I hope that your darling Catrina rots in hell!

Mrs. Mendez gasped. She had never seen Victoria so angry. How she had turned on her!

Mrs. Mendez waited and was almost sorry that she'd brought up the subject, but in her recent dream, she had seen a journal lying on a bedspread. It had opened by itself, but she couldn't make out what was written in it. Was it in Spanish? But, Mrs. Mendez could read Spanish quite well.

She heard Victoria's footsteps coming along the corridor. For some reason...nerves?...anticipation?...she found it difficult to breathe.

Victoria flung open the door and tossed the journal on to the bedspread...just as Mrs. Mendez had visualized it in her dream.

-Dear God!

-What is it, mother?

Victoria had calmed down, somewhat, to the point of being civil.

Mrs. Mendez moved her leg under the bedspread causing the journal to flip open. The matriarch was now terrified.

-Victoria, read it to me, *please*!

Victoria smiled with wicked satisfaction.

-Why should I?

-Victoria!

-Oh, very well, mother.

She picked up the journal and read its brief contents aloud.

"Victoria, my darling, when you read this, I will have been murdered for my past crimes. Take care...the end of the world is at hand and can only be prevented by a leap back in time atop the triangle.

"I love you."

And, with that, Victoria Mendez broke down and cried.

FIVE

OFFICER MARCO MORALES followed the young man to his apartment on the upper east side of Manhattan. It was a small apartment that consisted of a bedroom and a bathroom. The young man either had to eat his meals out or bring in a hot plate. Marco stood next to the bed because the young man had invited him in. He knew that he was being followed. He had expected it. He was glad that it was Officer Morales.

-I can speak English. They lied to you before and I was afraid to contradict them.

Marco sat on the bed next to the frightened young man. The Police Officer resisted putting his arm around the young man's shoulder

-Tell me the whole story...from the beginning. I won't betray this confidence to your friends.

-Friends? They are not my friends. We know each other and try to take advantage of each other...especially when one of us has money. You know how it is.

-I sure do. So, how did you happen to be in Columbus Circle this Monday?

-Nathan was telling the truth. It was an acting job...extras in some kind of feature documentary. We're Asian, so acting jobs don't come too often.

-What do you know about Roger Lee?

-He's dangerous. He'd sell his own mother to a pawn broker.

-Do you know him, personally?

-On occasion. He's...what do you call it? A switch hitter. He swings both ways.

Marco grinned at this bit of information about the hood.

-Didn't know that. Has he hit on you?

-Yes. And, that's how we got the jobs as extras..through my "friendship" with Roger.

-Now, it's beginning to come together. Keep talking and tell me everything you know about the infamous Mr. Roger Lee.

-He owns a lot of real estate in Chinatown, but he'd like to branch out. You know, mainstream stuff. At least, that's how he puts it.

-What kind of real estate?

-Nightclubs...they're his specialty. But, also saunas and a couple of restaurants. But, as I hear it, he's heavy in debt. Some say that he's even desperate for money. And, believer me, he'll do anything for it.

-Was he behind Susan Broder's kidnapping?

-I don't think so. He was contacted by somebody. I don't know who, and I might even be wrong about this. He doesn't tell me everything, you know. He doesn't trust anyone completely. He can't afford to.

-When are you gonna' see Mr. Roger Lee, again?

-That's up to him.

-Do you know how to contact him?

-No. At least not by phone. I know some of his favorite hangouts, though.

-Good. You got some paper and a pencil handy?

-Yes.

-I want you to write down for me every piece of real estate that Roger Lee owns or is associated with. And, then, tell me his favorite spots and favorite people.

Officer Morales left the young man to it and went into the bathroom to relieve himself. And, being of a curious mind, he had a look in the medicine cabinet. The shelves were lined with bottles of alcohol. He flushed the toilet and went back into the bedroom. The young man was still busy writing down names and addresses. Marco sat down next to him, again. He noticed that the walls in the apartment were bare...not so much as a postcard was affixed to the walls.

-You're being cooperative and that's good. It will go well with you.

The young man stopped writing and looked up at Marco with desperation in his eyes.

-Enough to keep me in this wonderful country? I am here illegally, you know.

Marco had guessed as much.

-We'll help you out. What's your name...your real name.

-Bao Liu...that is my real name. And, if you get Roger Lee, at least my life will be safe.

-Oh, we'll get Mr. Lee, all right...one way or another.

Ginny Gray was sitting at her desk and thinking about the events of the past few days. Her by-line had appeared under every headline from last Saturday to today's paper on the newsstand. Nice. And, finally a well deserved raise along with the recognition and respect that she so rightfully deserved. For the immediate future, life was sweet. However, one must not rest on one's laurels...that would be a fatal journalistic mistake.

Ginny stirred the sugar in her coffee. She looked about the newsroom. It had an almost cozy feel to it. But she quickly roused herself from this passive mood. This reporter had phone calls to make. Among those on her list were Edward Mendez, Manuel Mendez and Marlena Lake: three interesting people to say the least.

She dialed Edward's number first, but he wasn't in. His sister, Dottie, answered the call. Her brother wasn't out on any particular case as far as she knew. And, she had no idea when her detective brother would be back in the office.

Ginny next dialed Manuel Mendez's number. His manservant answered and said that his "master" could not be disturbed, but he would inform Mr. Mendez that Miss Gray had called.

Ginny dialed Marlena Lake's number and her daughter, Susan, answered.

-Susan! I finally got through to someone! How are you holding up?

-Just fine, Miss Gray. How are you?

-Name's Ginny. And, I'm just fine. How's Mom?

-Her usual self. Ginny, how can I help you?

-Well...is Marlena upset about that ransom money? I mean a quarter-of-a-million is a quarter-of-a-million. I'd be livid.

-She's not as upset as one might think. Money doesn't worry her...esoteric matters do...and a great deal.

Ginny smelled a story here. She tried to be subtle in her questions to the girl.

-Like what, babe?

-I'm not sure that I can answer that. Mother can be very secretive when it suits her.

-Do me a favor?

-If I can. You handled my kidnapping story with flare, but in good taste. Thank you.

-My pleasure. Now...just let me know who Marlena has contacted since your return. Who's she been on the phone with? Even better, who's been to her townhouse and who has she visited.

Susan caught her breath.

-You sound like Edward on one of his cases. As a matter of fact, he's been here twice since my "return."

-Good. Who else?

-Alexandra Raymond who only just left a short time ago. And-

-Yes? Don't hold out on me.

-Irene Wong is coming over. Their conversation over the phone sounded rather intense.

Ginny was positively delighted with this bit of news.

-And? There is more, isn't there? There has to be.

-Edward and Lt. Donovan just called. They're coming over, as well.

-What a cozy little group. Susan, I'll be blunt: what's up? You can tell me in the strictest confidence. You know that.

-It's pretty serious, Ginny. As serious as when the sun disappeared. I can't say anymore. I'm sorry that I can't.

-I can. I have other sources, Susan. And, I happen to know it's about the end of the world.

Doomsday

Mabel Scott was the proud owner of a three story apartment building on Sullivan St., just off the SoHo district in Manhattan. Her late husband had purchased it just after the Great War: W.W. I, it was now called. He got a veteran's loan from the bank, hocked a few family heirlooms and made a substantial down payment. The building had been paid off while Wilbur Scott was still alive. He died a happy man knowing that he'd left his wife well provided for.

On this Wednesday in late May, Mabel had been sweeping the first floor hallway when she saw Edward Mendez coming from Lorraine Keyes's second floor apartment. Mabel liked her pretty tenant. The girl was a well mannered and soft spoken young lady who always had a kind word for her landlady. Mabel had recognized Edward from his newspaper photos. She was impressed that one of her tenants knew the celebrated detective. She saw that Lorraine wasn't...shall one say?...fully dressed...wearing only her slip. So, she decided to wait for a more appropriate time to quiz the girl about her shamus visitor.

Mabel moved on to the second floor. She finished her sweeping there and continued on to the third floor and that's when the front door opened. At first, Mabel thought nothing of it. Probably one of her tenants coming in. She continued with her sweeping, but she did hear the footsteps on the stairwell. Still, it didn't concern her. The footsteps stopped in front of Lorraine's door. Mabel heard the muffled creak of the door being opened...but, no one had bothered to knock. Was it Mr. Mendez returning? She didn't think so. But, she didn't want to take a chance on missing the detective. She put down her broom and dust pan and quietly descended the stairs. She was halfway down when she heard Lorraine scream. Mabel hurried down the flight of stairs and banged on the girl's door.

-Lorraine! Lorraine! Are you all right, dear?

Mabel tried the door, but it was locked. She heard another scream that was abruptly cut short.

-Help! Someone help!

Mabel banged on Lorraine's door once more and, then, gave it up. She ran down the flight of stairs and out on to the stoop. She screamed for the police...for anyone to help.

A movement behind her caught her attention.

-Oh, my God!

A man in a black suit was dangling from the second story window of Lorraine's apartment. He was there for only a split second before he dropped to the ground, landing nimbly on his feet. He looked at Mabel and, then, bolted across the street and into a dark sedan. He pulled out of the parking space and sped down the street and out of sight.

By this time, Mabel had gathered her wits and went next door to use her neighbor's phone to call the police.

Doomsday

Why had no one answered her calls for help? Were people so insensitive or just plain scared?

SIX

-I DON'T know how long I have.

-We will help you, Miss Wong. I am not without resources and connections.

-I hope that you're right. I know that my life is in danger. Roger Lee will not rest until I am dead. I know that. I betrayed him and he will never forgive me for that.

-Leave Mr. Lee to Edward Mendez's capable hands. He is your friend as I and my daughter are.

-Thank you.

-More tea, my dear?

-Yes. Thank you. It's very good.

Marlena poured more tea for Miss Wong and added a slice of lemon to the beautiful girl's beverage.

Susan came back into the room and was surprised to see Miss Irene Wong.

-Oh, Miss Wong. I didn't know that you arrived.

-Yes. A few minutes ago. Are you well, Miss Lake?

Doomsday

-It's Miss Broder. And, please, call me Susan. I think we've earned the right to be on a first name basis, don't you.?

-Absolutely. Please, sit next to me.

-I will.

-Tea, Susan?

-Why, thank you, mother. What have you two been discussing?

-Just observing the preliminary civilities.

Susan smiled and accepted the proffered tea cup.

Miss Wong spoke up in earnest. She had had enough with the civilities.

-Perhaps, we should get to the heart of the matter?

Marlena lit a cigar and sat back in her armchair.

-Yes. Let's.

-Miss Lake? Susan? The deceased Professor Lange was concerned about the effect of the sun's disappearance on the Earth's orbit.

-We're quite aware of that, Miss Wong. It has concerned me for several years now. It has never left my thoughts.

-You're an intelligent woman, Miss Lake. The Earth's orbit has shifted and the shift is increasing with each passing day.

-Indeed. It's as I feared.

-It must be corrected. The Earth must be brought back to its original elliptical orbit or we will all be doomed.

Susan put down her tea cup. She shrugged her shoulders in frustration.

-How? Isn't that the question we're all asking?

Marlena let out a puff of aromatic smoke.

-My daughter comes straight to the point. And, she is quite right to do so. We've no time to waste on trifles.

-Professor Gerald Lawrence has one solution in mind.

Marlena leaned forward in her chair. She was keenly interested in men of science and their accomplishments. She had a great respect for science and knowledge.

-I know that name. He's quite respected in his field of astronomy if I'm not mistaken.

-Yes. He is most respected.

Susan addressed Irene to ask the ultimate question...a question that she was almost afraid to ask.

-What's his solution...or dare one ask?

It was Irene's turn to put down her tea cup.

-A hydrogen blast near the Antarctic region...several such simultaneous detonations would be necessary.

Susan suppressed a gasp. Marlena choked on her cigar smoke...even she was taken aback. Irene couldn't help but smile, but there was no pleasure in that smile.

-I know. It is pretty drastic, no? But, we have been hard pressed for a better solution if there is any.

Marlena sufficiently recovered herself to voice her objections to Professor Lawrence's plan.

-But, the damage caused by such atomic detonations would be catastrophic. It might do more harm than good, if it even works. And, I'm not convinced that it would work. Susan, what do you think, dear?

-Frankly, as a last resort...maybe. Irene, were any other possibilities mentioned?

-No. None. How does one go about moving a planet? But, the hydrogen blasts would cause at least a minor tilt in the Earth's axis and that would in effect trigger a planetary shift.

Marlena put out her cigar and smirked at what she had just heard.

-You hope. I think there's more risk than promise. I don't like Professor Lawrence's so-called solution.

Susan agreed with her mother.

-It is pretty frightening. My God, it could all backfire. And, how do we stop the Earth's movement? Isn't space a void...a vacuum? Once the planet is shifted, how do you stop it? It could careen toward the sun.

Marlena agreed with her daughter.

-A ghastly thought..to be cremated alive. Horrible!

Irene spoke with some trepidation. She felt that she had to defend Professor Lawrence.

-I, myself, have a solution to the obstacle that Susan just mentioned...in theory, of course.

-What's your theory, Irene?

-The moon would act as a buffer. The gravity that the moon exerts upon the Earth could be used to stop the Earth from moving toward the sun. It could be done. I'm sure of it. The timing and location of the hydrogen blasts would have to be precise...most precise.

Marlena sat back, shaking her head.

-Risky. Too many unknown variables. Oh, I'm not criticizing you, Miss Wong, or Professor Lawrence...quite the contrary.. But, what of the radiation fall-out and the effects on the Antarctic ice sheets?

Irene reached into her purse for her compact. She needed a distraction...a trivial and feminine distraction.

-I know. But, what else can we do? What's the alternative? We must do something. We can't just sit around and accept our fate.

-Are the governments of our world informed of this? They must be by this time.

-Yes. And, they are trying to keep it "top secret." But, already it's starting to leak out.

-And, worldwide panic is the last thing we need.

That was Susan who addressed her mother.

-Mother? I can see the wheels turning in that brain of yours.

-We must find another solution. I don't like what I've just heard. I don't like it at all.

-Miss Lake, that's why I've come here today. My calculations are incomplete. I need to see Professor Lange's notes. Can you arrange that for me?

-Of course. We must go there at once. There is no time to-

There was a knock on the front door and everyone in the room started.

-That's probably Edward. He practically never uses the doorbell. Susan, dear, let the dear boy in, would you. I was just about to mention his very name.

Susan got up to answer the doorbell and to her immense pleasure it was the P. I. And, standing beside him was none other than Lt. William Donovan.

-Hello, Susan.

-Edward, please come in. And, you, too, Lt. Donovan.

-Thank you, Miss Broder.

-Not at all.

Edward led the way into the living room followed by the Lieutenant and Susan.

-Edward, dear boy, please sit down. I've saved your usual seat for you. Lt. Donovan, please sit next to Miss Wong.

Susan mixed Edward his usual Scotch and soda and, then, turned to the Lieutenant.

-Lt. Donovan? May I pour you a drink?

-Club soda, thanks.

-Of course. You're on duty.

Marlena took over the gathering in her usual manner.

-I'm afraid we must dispense with the pleasantries and apprise Edward and the Lieutenant of the current situation.

Susan handed Edward and Lt. Donovan their respective drinks.

Marlena continued to address her audience with earnest.

-Edward? Lt. Donovan? The Earth is slowly drifting into deep space. This must be corrected and thus far the only solution seems to be a rather drastic one. Miss Wong, perhaps, you'd like to explain?

Irene rose to the task and made it brief and simple. The two men in the room stared fixedly at the scientist.

-Well, gentlemen, what do you think?

Lt. Donovan shook his head in dismay.

-Miss Lake, it sounds like we're blowing up the world to save it. It's insane even if it works.

Edward finished his drink and placed it on the coffee table.

-I'm with the Lieutenant on that one. But, putting my monumental doubts aside for the moment, what's the timeline on this H-bomb plan?

Irene answered the P. I. and there was urgency in her voice...and fear.

-The plan can be executed no later that June 21st the Summer Solstice. It must be no later than that date or it will be too late. The elliptical plane will be in the optimal position until then and no later. There is no other way...something must be done and there's no alternate plan. Yes, Lt. Donovan?

-Who else knows about this doomsday we're facing? We just got a telex. this morning putting my Precinct on stand-by alert. Why, Miss Wong? It's been two and a half years since the sun took a powder so what the hell's the rush?

-The deadline has to be met. And, quite frankly, we're not certain of the effects of the hydrogen detonations.

-Meaning that if the drift into space doesn't eventually kill us, the H-bombs will.

-I confess to the possibility.

The Lieutenant was getting heated. Edward decided to run interference for Irene before things flared up into an argument.

-Okay, so we've got about three weeks to play with. The world's governments are keeping the lid on this, right, Irene?

-Yes. But, too many people had to be told in order to make preparations. It couldn't be helped.

Edward asked Susan for a refill. He continued to think in a sort of stream-of-consciousness mode.

-Let me do some reconnoitering. Maybe...just maybe...we can come up with an alternate plan...'cause, baby, this one sounds like a suicide mission that even a kamikaze pilot wouldn't take on.

Susan handed Edward his Scotch and soda....a double. He needed it. And, she wouldn't mind one herself.

-Thanks, baby. Anyway, to change the subject, Lt. Donovan has something to show you Marlena.

-Please.

Lt. Donovan took out the envelope and handed it to Marlena.

-Miss Lake, can you make any sense of this?

Marlena read it with interest...and, then, read it through, once again.

-Yes. It's meaning is clear enough...to me, but who sent it?

-We were hoping that you could tell us, Miss Lake.

-The Flatiron Building is in the form of a triangle: the magical symbol for material manifestation.

Lt. Donovan smiled. He was not at all surprised by this woman's knowledge.

-Miss Lake, please go on.

-The script...the font...

Edward cut in.

-We've seen it before, Marlena.

Marlena handed the note to Susan.

-Mother, it's from one of those books we appropriated from that house in Staten Island. I think it's the one on quantum mechanics.

-Yes! Good girl. That was also my impression. Miss Wong will you stay the night? We'll need your mathematical genius.

-Of course. I'll have to stop by my place and pick up a few things, if you don't mind.

-I won't hear of it. Anything you may need is here. And, what isn't, we can send out for.

Marlena turned back to the two men.

-Edward, you'll let me know what you turn up. And, Lieutenant? I would pay a visit to the roof of the Flatiron Building if I were you. Someone or persons familiar with magic...complex ritual magic...and science is making preparations for some kind of manifestation or, possibly, even time travel.

-Marlena, what about Professor Lange's notes?

-I doubt that we'll need them now, Miss Wong, but...

Marlena turned to the Lieutenant with an inquiry.

-Lt. Donovan? Could you access Professor Lange's notes for us? The notes could provide an alternate plan.

-We'll subpoena them. Might take a couple of days, though.

-Make it one day, Lieutenant. We are in a hurry.

Edward and the Lt. Donovan were standing outside Marlena's townhouse. It was just past two in the afternoon.

-Well, Mendez, where you off to on this sunny and brisk day? Got a lot to think about.

-I'll say! I'm heading into Brooklyn to pay my mother a visit.

-Interesting lady, your Mom.

-Yes. Tomorrow...well, I'll be visiting my erstwhile father.

-Interesting family, you've got.

-You're being kind, Lieutenant. Don't have to be. What are your plans?

-I'm on my way to the Flatiron Building. That is, after I stop off at the 86th and get on to that subpoena. You know, I've never been inside that building.

-Neither have I.

A moment of silence fell between the two men. It was almost a relief from the tension of the afternoon.

-Hey, Mendez, did you know that Professor Lange's apartment on the east side is still vacant and the lease was renewed by a Miss Mary Riley.

The P. I. laughed.

-Well, what do you know? Maybe, I'll pay Miss Riley a visit tomorrow, as well.

Edward stopped off at his downtown office to check on any phone calls or visitors he might have missed. Dottie filled him in.

-Keven Evers called and asked for an appointment.

-Not this week. Monday. Tell him Monday.

-Our sister, Victoria, called. She sounded quite upset, but she wouldn't give me the details. I guess she doesn't trust me.

-That's it?

-Not quite. Det. Adam Kinsella dropped by.
-No kidding. What did Adam want?
-Here.

Dottie handed Edward a set of car keys.

-You mean he drove my DeSoto in from Long Island? Now, there's a buddy for you. But, how does he plan on getting back to the sticks?

-He doesn't. He's staying with Marco at his place and they'll be taking Marco's jeep back to Smithtown late Friday night. He couldn't hang around here, but he didn't say why. Oh! And, your brand new, repaired car is parked on the corner of John St. and Broadway. It's the closest parking space he could find.

-That's pretty damned close. At last, some good news.

-What do you mean, "at last?"

-Let's call it a day. I'll drive you home and fill you in on doomsday.

-You're on.

Dottie grabbed her handbag and sweater and waited for her brother at the door. Edward shut the lights and locked up.

SEVEN

LT. WILLIAM DONOVAN drove downtown to the Flatiron Building on 23rd St. and Broadway. It was one of the original skyscrapers in New York City. Its history was not a very pleasant one. A garment fire on one of its upper floors had caused the death of several young women. It had made the local papers for weeks and put the safety of skyscrapers into serious question for a time.

Lt. Donovan parked his car across the street from his destination and made his way to the skyscraper. The interior was faded art-deco and the elevators were manually operated with all of the old fashioned grill work still in place. It was a long wait, but the elevator finally arrived. He got in.

-Top floor, please.

-Yes, sir.

The ride up was slow but steady. Lt. Donovan got out and made his way down the narrow corridor. His footsteps made clicking noises and for some reason, he sensed that he was the only person on that floor.

He reached the door marked, "To roof." He opened the door and climbed the stairwell to the rooftop. He opened that door and walked out on to the tarmac.

-Good afternoon, Lieutenant. I was expecting my son, Edward Mendez, but your company is not unwelcome.

-What are you doing up here, Mr. Mendez?

-You and I and my son have business up here...or will have.

-You sent me that note?

-I sent that instruction. Yes. Come, Lt. Donovan, look at this impressive view of Manhattan. How it's changed in the last fifty years; from the primitive to the modern.

Lt. Donovan walked over to where Manuel Mendez stood. The view was spectacular. He could see straight down Broadway and get a glimpse of lower Manhattan. However, none of this interested the Lieutenant. He turned to face Edward's father.

-What's your game, Mr. Mendez?

-I don't play the usual "games." I play "games" of logic and abstraction.

-Why do you want me and your son up here this Friday? What the hell good would that do?

-You come directly to the purpose. The two of you will be, in a sense, humanity's hired assassins.

-Keep talking.

Manuel Mendez nodded approval at Lt. Donovan's response.

-Good. That does not shock you. I am aware of Professor Gerald Lawrence's plan to "save" mankind. It is a complete and utter folly. The end result will only succeed in annihilating mankind in the most horrific way.

Lt. Donovan grinned more to himself than to Mr. Mendez.

-You got a better plan up your sleeve?

-Yes. And, a rather brilliant one. If it works – and that will depend on you and my son – it will solve the riddle of time.

Manuel Mendez stopped for a moment to let his words sink in. He continued.

-Professor Lawrence and Miss Wong's "plan" could actually work, but it could alter the planet's axis. And, those two scientists are missing the picture in its entirety.

-How do you mean? What are they missing?

-When the sun "slipped" into another dimension, it not only affected the Earth's orbit, but also that of the other planets, as well.

Lt. Donovan was beginning to understand.

-So, even if we...

-Yes, Lieutenant. Even if this suicide plan of theirs succeeds, it will not place the other planets back into their proper position...specifically, Mercury and Venus: the two inner planets. And, to a lesser extent, the orbits of Mars and the outer planets have also been affected, but they pose no threat for us.

-Let me ask you this: if we correct the Earth's orbit, what happens to Mercury and Venus.

-Slowly, they will careen from the sun and cause gravitational disturbances

-You mean they could collide with the Earth?

-That's not been calculated. Their closer proximity to the Earth would be enough to cause massive upheavals in the tectonic plates and the very atmosphere...doomsday would be merely delayed.

The Lieutenant took out a cigarette and tapped it on the pack.

-Okay. So, getting back to me and your son, Edward, how do we figure into your plan?

-You will be sent back in time to make certain that the sun's disappearance *never* occurs. You will, in effect, change the course of history...or at least a part of it.

-And, just how the hell do we do all this? It can't be done.

The Lieutenant lit his cigarette and took a drag. Manuel Mendez looked Lt. Donovan straight in the eye as the latter blew smoke in his face.

-It can and *will* be done. On Friday, I will explain it all in detail. And, if you are unwilling, Lt. Donovan, then choose another to take your place.

Edward was having an after dinner drink with his mother and three sisters. He told them about Yolanda's phone call that morning and all four ladies were properly shocked by the news.

-I liked that girl, Edward. She had good old-fashioned spunk. I'm sorry and disappointed in her reasoning. She may one day come to regret her decision.

Dottie spoke up, waving her cigarette about in the air.

-I'm with you, mother. Too bad...for her, that is.

Victoria was more sympathetic to the figure skater.

-I'm not saying that I like what she did. I don't. But, as a woman, I can understand her motives.

Dottie turned on her sister. She didn't like dissension in the family ranks.,

-I don't. And, how long has she known this Brazilian coffee magnate? Not that long, I bet.

Edward shrugged his broad shoulders, trying not to give a damn.

-Not long...unless she was holding out on me.

Nella spoke with blunt honesty in her quiet way.

-Yolanda was nice, but an opportunist, I'm afraid. Is that being unkind? I don't mean to be.

Dottie laughed out loud. She appreciated Nella's remark.

-It happens to be true. Don't apologize for speaking the truth, Nella.

Edward finished his Scotch and soda. He turned the conversation to another topic.

-Mother?

-Yes, Edward? What's on your mind?

-Dottie's filled you in on the coming apocalypse.

It was not a question.

-Yes. She has.

-What do you and my father know about it? I'll rephrase that last question. What in God's name can be done about it?

-You've read the message in Victoria's journal, Edward.

-Before dinner. Victoria showed it to me and it corroborates with the note that Lt. Donovan received today.

-What note is that?

-A note written in "future" type from an anonymous sender who might be my father.

Nella asked an obvious question.

-Why the Flatiron Building? Because of its triangular shape and location?

Mrs. Mendez took it upon herself to answer.

-Most likely. Your father once had an office on the top floor of that very building.

-Then, that *was* his note.

-I think Eddie's right.

-Thanks, Dottie. So...what does my dear Dad know that we don't? Mother? You want to tell us?

Mrs. Mendez finished her tea with a sigh of satisfaction.

-As you know Edward, he was the leader of an occult group. I was told that his magical abilities were impressive and even frightening.

-Why frightening, mother?

-Because, Nella, he acquired many of his abilities from the Mexican oracles. As a young man, he often visited that country. It changed him. For a time, he became addicted to peyote...a narcotic that was supposed to enhance one's consciousness and to actually displace...separate it from one's body to any point in the fifth dimension of time. Your father often said that he could see the "grid" that held the visual world together. He could travel along these lines...suspend himself in mid-air if he chose and render himself invisible. His followers feared him as well they should have.

-And, he obtained these powers from?

-Yes, Edward, he obtained them from an ancient seer. I don't know the name or if he even has a name. Does it matter?

Edward shook his head and got up to get a refill.

-No. Not at the moment, anyway. But, getting back to this "grid," what is it?

Nella answered his question.

-Would it be like the lines on a sheet of graph paper? Lines used in geometry and calculus?

Doomsday

Mrs. Mendez was impressed with her daughter's knowledge of the occult and its links to science.

-Yes, my dear, that's a very apt analogy. The purity of mathematics...the vibratory power of numbers. It's progressed to quantum physics, if the German physicists can be relied upon.

Edward, refill in hand, leaned forward in his chair.

-Where do these grid lines lead to?

-Infinity and even beyond that finite concept.

-When you get on one of these grid lines, how do you get off? Can you get off?

-I've no idea, Edward. Your father only shared his general knowledge with me. The actual workings...the mechanics, if you would, were only taught to another initiate, if he were worthy...very few were.

Edward sat back and took a sip of his drink.

-Well, I'll have to ask father about this. Maybe, he'll tell me. Who knows? But, I do know that he wants me for something.

Victoria spoke up. Talk of the occult frightened her...and so did her father.

-Edward, be careful I fear that our father is a dangerous man and not to be trusted...at least, not entirely.

Dottie got up and went over to the drinks table.

-Refill, anyone?

Edward wanted another drink and so did Dottie. That's why she got up in the first place.

Roger Lee sat back in the fake leather chair with a rather thoughtful expression on his handsome face. He was holding his tea cup close to his lips. The green tea was cold, but that was the way he liked it...cold and bitter. He was sitting in his favorite Chinese restaurant right in the heart of Chinatown just one block north of the Civic Center. The chair opposite him was vacant and pushed against the table's edge. He wasn't expecting anyone because he had no real friends to speak of. He had underground contacts and enemies...men and women who feared and yet respected the Chinese gangster. He was a fair man in his own way, but ruthless.

The restaurant was dark with recessed red lighting. The tables were not covered with any kind of tablecloths, but every object was impeccably clean. It could not be otherwise because Roger Lee owned this restaurant even though it was under another man's name.

At this moment, Roger Lee was satisfied with the recent turn of events even though he, himself, had had a "close shave" with the law. Two of his associates were now lying on cement slabs in the city morgue. The half-a-million had been delivered to Manuel Mendez and Roger had been given his twenty percent cut of the money. Yes. A good haul. That kind of money would last him for quite a long time...long enough to get him to Hong Kong safely and...to murder Irene Wong...the double-crossing bitch who would get what was coming to her. He would see to that. A silk chord around her neck, perhaps, or a permanent dive into the Hudson River. So many possibilities. And, of course, one could not rule out a slow and painful torture.

Roger Lee smiled and finished his tea. He signaled the waiter for a check. He always paid even though he had no reason to. It kept the bookkeeping straight and honest. It also kept the I.R.S off his back.

He got up and put on his Fedora and left the restaurant. He walked down the narrow stairs and out into the late evening of this rather chilly May day. He knew that the police were still looking for him so he made it a practice to mingle with the crowd...and in Chinatown that was quite easy. He knew that people recognized him, but he was confident of their silence.

Who was that blonde woman up ahead? It was Connie Fulton. Roger Lee made no attempt to either follow her or be noticed. He knew all too well where she lived and worked. He owned the place He knew where her girlfriend, Miss Irene Wong, lived, as well. Would Irene have moved by now? If she were smart, yes. But, maybe not. Irene was curiously naive in matters of survival and strategy. Nevertheless, Roger Lee didn't dare go anywhere near her apartment. For sure, the cops would be on the look-out for him. They'd even have an eye on Connie. Both of those women could wait. Roger Lee was in no great hurry.

Slowly...casually...Roger Lee made his way to his apartment complex that was just one block outside of Chinatown. It was a new and modern equipped building. The exterior was white brick which was already turning gray from city pollution. It was ten stories tall with an elevator system and an elaborate fire alarm system...but no doorman. If there had been one, Roger Lee would not have taken his third floor apartment.

He entered the building and climbed the two flights of stairs instead of taking the elevator. The climb was good for his heart and leg muscles. When he came out on to his floor, he turned right, walked down the brightly lit corridor and stopped in front of Apt. 3E. He took out his house keys and let himself in. He switched on the lights. The room was furnished in the "modern style" of the 1950's: pastel colors for the "light" furniture and wall-to-wall carpeting in a soft, dove gray.

Roger Lee plopped down on to the sofa. The envelope on the coffee table caught his eye. He reached over and tore it open. He took out the note. It read:

"They are so easily deceived. Perhaps, it's their desperation. Yes. That would account for it.

"Mr. Roger Lee be at the Flatiron Building before sunrise this Friday on the 27th. Me and my son, Edward, will be there. Do not fail me. An additional $50,000 will be paid to you upon completion of the enormous task ahead of you. If for any reason you cannot be there, inform me at once"

Doomsday

It was signed Mr. Mendez

Roger Lee picked up a book of matches. He lit one and burned both paper and envelope. He let the ashes burn out in the ashtray on the coffee table.

-Fifty grand, pal? It had better be one hundred grand to make it worth my while. I like round numbers. And, don't think that I don't know what you're up to. You want a hired assassin...fair enough. Let's just hope that your son doesn't get in my way.

Part II
Miss Lorraine Keyes

ONE

EDWARD MENDEZ sat in his mother's kitchen at the breakfast table with his two sisters, Dottie and Nella. His cheese omelet was half eaten. He held his coffee cup in his right hand. He took his coffee black with no sugar. Nella got up to get her brother more toast. Dottie was reading the morning paper. The lead story was about a pretty young blonde who had been murdered near Little Italy on Sullivan St. The P. I. had not yet seen the headline. Dottie read on.

"Late Wednesday morning, Lorraine Keyes was brutally murdered in her Sullivan St. apartment. The suspect was seen leaving in a daring escape...climbing down the front of the building. The suspect ran across the street and into his car...fleeing the scene of the crime. There were no witnesses except for the building's landlady who did not get a good look at the suspect...only that he was tall and wearing a black suit and sunglasses.

"Miss Keyes was last seen in the company of Edward Mendez, P. I. who is not a suspect in the case."

Dottie stopped reading and handed the paper to Edward.

-You'd better read this for yourself.

Edward did just that and held his temper in check.

-Why haven't the cops been in touch with me? I'm definitely on their people of interest check-list.

Edward handed the paper to Nella. Dottie was studying her brother's reaction.

-Stops staring at me, Dottie. I don't like it.

-Sorry. But, Eddie, you're a hard man to get a hold of. Maybe, the police have been trying to get in touch. We did leave the office early yesterday.

-Maybe. I'd better stop off at the 6th Precinct House as soon as I leave here.

-You want company?

-No, thanks, Dottie. You head on over to the office and hold down the fort. You don't mind taking the train, do you?

-Not a bit.

Nella finished reading the article and put the paper down on to the table.

-Edward, the black suit and sunglasses...it wouldn't be...

The P. I. grinned at his sister and the question.

-One of Romo-Ark's boys? Probably following me. But, why kill the girl?

Nella continued to probe.

-When did you meet Miss Keyes?

-At that small eatery right outside Chinatown, Sam's Bar n' Grill. Why?

-Had you met her before?

-You mean before yesterday? No. Yes. Sort of. A couple of years back, we spotted each other on the subway. It was the day the sun disappeared. What are you hinting at, Nella? You think it's some kind of a set-up?

-It wouldn't be the first time. What stop did the girl get off?

-Beats me. I got off before she did at Fulton St.

Nella buttered her toast and took a bite.

-You know that I don't believe in coincidence. I think it was a set-up, Edward. It was planned and for what purpose, I don't know.

Edward was incredulous.

-You mean you think the girl worked for Romo-Ark?

-Yes. I do. They're too cunning not to employ girls.

Edward finished his toast and omelet not really tasting much of anything. He left for the 6th Precinct House lighting a cigarette.

Doomsday

-Cherie? More coffee? It is quite good this morning. I've already had two cups myself.

-Thanks you, Nathalie. Yes. Another cup would be nice.

Nathalie Montaigne poured her long time friend, Werner Hoffman, another cup of steaming hot coffee in the over-sized white porcelain cup.

-Cream?

-No. I want to savor the coffee in its pure state.

-As you wish.

-Nathalie, have you read the morning paper?

-No. Not yet. Why do you ask?

-Two interesting articles you might like to read.

-Tell me.

-One involves your friend, Edward Mendez.

-Oh? How so?

-He was the last person to be seen in the company of a murdered young girl, Lorraine Keyes.

-The girl's name means nothing to me.

-It rings a bell in my mind.

-Did you know her?

-No. But, somewhere...someone mentioned her name in passing.

-Who?

Werner Hoffman shrugged his shoulders.

-If I could remember, I would tell you. I must think upon it.

He drank his coffee, savoring the strong flavor.

-Nathalie...this is delicious coffee.

-Isn't it? And, Werner, the other story of interest?

-The American Museum of Natural History has an interesting exhibit opening up this coming Autumn.

-Please, don't keep me in suspense.

-Certain ancient Sumerian artifacts will be on display...artifacts that date back nearly 6,000 years.

-Such as? You have my complete attention, cherie.

-An urn...a small ceremonial urn and a necklace...which was donated by a man who chooses to remain anonymous.

-We must go to this exhibit, by all means.

-I knew that you'd want to, so I've arranged to be invited to a private showing...just prior to the public display.

-You have connections, still, Werner.

-Yes.

-And, what else, cherie?

-I mean to have those object for my own collection.

Doomsday

TWO

EDWARD MENDEZ was sitting across from Detective Hopper of the 6th Precinct House which was just two blocks south of where Lorraine Keyes had been murdered. The Precinct was smaller that the 86th; consisting only of a main floor and a second floor that housed the Interrogation Rooms, restrooms and a couple of shared offices. There was, of course, the basement which contained filing cabinets crammed with police records and ongoing cases and "cold" cases which were better known as "unsolved" cases. The Precinct House was kept clean and there was a certain order to the seeming chaos.

Detective Hopper's desk was the new kind of hard, thick metal: a dark gray. Edward didn't like it. It was too utilitarian and just plain ugly.

Detective Hopper was a handsome man: red hair and blue eyes and lean...maybe just a little too lean. He also smoked like a chimney. He offered Edward a cigarette.

-No. Thanks. I've got my own.

-Lucky Strike. Any good?

-Smooth taste.

-Mine's Chesterfield.

Both men lit up. A good smoke was just what they needed. It gave them something in common

-Well, Mr. Mendez, I appreciate your coming in. Mind you, you've been just about cleared by Miss Keyes's landlady. She seems to admire you.

-I'm duly grateful.

-But, we would like your take on Miss Keyes.

-I can't tell you all that much about her. I spotted her once on the subway a couple of years back. And, then, again, only yesterday.

-How was she yesterday?

-Fine. In good spirits, as far as I could tell.

-Did she drop any names?

Edward shook his head in the negative.

-No. None that I can remember. And, I would remember something like that.

-Did you have sex with her?

-I did. And, she wasn't half bad.

-Where'd you pick her up?

-Just off of Chinatown in a bar and grill that I frequent: Sam's Bar n' Grill. She came by my table and sat down.

-What did you talk about?

Edward shook his head and let out some cigarette smoke.

-How we happened to see each other on that subway train and neither one of us making a move. And, not much else.

Edward took another drag on his cigarette.

-Detective? I've been wondering about this man in a black suit.

-What about it?

-Well, if it hadn't been for him, it would have been a perfect set-up for yours truly sitting here.

-How do you mean?

-I would have been the last one seen coming out of her apartment. That goon comes climbing down the front of her building in plain sight of the whole damned neighborhood. Why? A hack writer from Hollywood could have written a better scene. What was the damned hurry in killing her? And, why the girl? Why not me?

Detective Hopper took a drag on his cigarette before responding.

-I'll bite.

-That goon was from Romo-Ark. You can bet your last paycheck on it. The question is, Detective Hopper, who exactly was Miss Lorraine Keyes? What's her background?

-We're checking on that now.

-And, we must have been followed back to her apartment.

-You're assuming that, Mendez. He might have been lying in wait for the girl.

-It's a pretty safe assumption. I'm sure I'm number one on Romo-Ark's most wanted list. Christ! They must hate my guts.

-But, as I said, they might have been keeping an eye on the girl.

-Why? I need a reason.

Detective Hopper shrugged noncommittally.

-It's too early in the game yet. Give us time, Mendez.

Edward put out his cigarette. Detective Hopper did likewise, but reached for another one.

-Could it have been a warning for you, Mendez?

-For what? Stay away from what or whom? I just don't get it.

Detective Hopper lit his cigarette.

-Could that Romo-Ark man have been a boyfriend of Miss Keyes's?

-Those creeps don't have girlfriends. But..I guess you can't rule it out. And, what about the landlady? What was her take on Lorraine?

-Nice girl, so she said. Kept to herself, but was friendly enough. Never saw too many men go up...until you showed up, that is.

-How long had she been living there?

-A couple of years. Paid the rent on time. Kept the apartment neat. Never made any demands on the landlady. In short, she minded her own damned business.

-And, before she lived there?

-We're checking on it.

-Let me know, will you? I feel kind of responsible for all this. It's like I was the trigger mechanism for her murder.

-We did find a set of keys in her place. The old fashioned kind that you see in Gothic mysteries. They wouldn't fit into most modern locks.

-Any way of tracing them?

To Edward's surprise, Detective Hopper took a set of keys out of his desk drawer and handed them to the P. I. The keys were on an over sized, brass key ring.

-Is this it?

-Yep. It's been tested for prints. Only Miss Keyes's were on it, we assume. We're still running a check through the F.B.I.

Edward held it up and stared at it. He was more perplexed than ever. What the hell did these keys open doors to?

Edward left the 6th Precinct with mixed feelings. It was a murder case, something that he could dig right into. It was something that didn't involve the end of the world or occultism. It was a down-to-earth murder of a pretty girl that he'd picked up and slept with.

He crossed the street and got into his DeSoto. He pulled out of his parking space and headed toward midtown, specifically the Flatiron Building. It was a reconnaissance mission in preparation for tomorrow. Traffic was light at this time of the morning so the P. I. arrived at 23rd St. and Broadway in just under ten minutes. He drove around looking for a parking space, but couldn't find any. Hmm. He decided that he'd wasted enough time and headed uptown...but, a pedestrian walking down 6th Ave caught his attention. There was something familiar about this man. Yes. The man looked like his father, Manuel Mendez.

-I'll just bet he's headed for the Flatiron Building.

Edward made an illegal U-turn and headed back to 23rd St. He had to be certain that it was his father. He saw the man entering the Flatiron Building.

-Bull's eye!

A car was pulling out of a parking space and Edward beat another car to it. He ignored the other driver's cursing and parked his DeSoto. He got out of the car and ran toward the entrance of the Flatiron Building. He flung open the the glass door and headed straight for the elevator bank. The man he spotted was standing there waiting for an elevator to arrive. He turned to face the P. I.

And, for a moment, the two men stared at each other.

-Hello, Edward.

The P. I. didn't respond.

-I am your father, Manuel Mendez.

-Hello, father.

The two men got into the elevator together and rode up to the top floor. Neither man said a word to the other. The elevator operator seemed to respect their muted silence. All three men stared straight ahead, barely moving a muscle. The upward trip was a long one, but it did, at last, come to a halt on the 22nd floor.

-Top floor.

-Thank you.

-Thank you.

Manuel Mendez and Edward Mendez stepped off the elevator and on to the 22nd floor. The father led the way down the corridor to an office on the right. The frosted glass window was blank. It had only the room number stenciled on it:Room 2243. Edward thought that an odd number. How could there be 43 offices on one floor in such a narrow building?

The two men entered the small office which was practically devoid of any furniture. There was only a mahogany desk and chair and a chair for the expected visitor. That's all. No filing cabinets, no rugs or even Venetian blinds on the one window in the room.

Manuel Mendez sat behind the desk and beckoned his son to have a seat. By reflex, Edward turned to flip on the light switch, but the overhead light did not come on.

-I had it disconnected. Only natural light will enter this room.

Edward sat down and took out a cigarette.

-May I smoke?

-Of course.

Edward lit up. Manuel Mendez produced a ceramic ashtray from a desk drawer and placed it in front of the P. I..

-Thanks.

-Don't mention it.

Edward took a deep drag on his Lucky Strike and began the conversation. He tried the direct approach.

-Okay. Why am I here?

-You get straight to the purpose, shamus. Tomorrow, you and Lt. William Donovan will make quite a daring attempt to save this planet of ours.

-And, just how are we supposed to do that...assuming it can be done?

-In any experiment, there is a risk. But, I'm confident that it can be done.

-Is this an experiment?

Manuel Mendez sat back in his chair. He folded his arms across his chest.

-It is a mission. You and the Lieutenant are to travel back in time to avert the sun's disappearance on that fateful day in December of 1947.

Edward flicked some ash into the ceramic ashtray.

Doomsday

-You lost me. How do we travel back in time and how in hell do we prevent a horde of Nazis from doing what they did down in the Antarctic? We'd be changing history and every event that followed. Your plan is as nutty as Irene Wong's.

Manuel Mendez leaned forward in his chair, earnestly trying to convince his son of the validity of his daring plan..

-No. You are wrong, Edward. You would only be changing that "fragment"...that particular "piece" of history and nothing else.

-You don't know that. You can't possibly know that. You're theorizing. It's just guess work. Right?

-You are challenging me? Good. I would do the same.

Manuel Mendez leaned even further forward in his chair. He now placed both arms on the mahogany desk.

-You and Lt. Donovan will target the scientist and the two engineers responsible for the obscenity that they executed. No trip to the south pole will be necessary. The two men and one woman will be in New York City when you arrive in the past. It should be easy pickings for you.

-Two time travelers. Two hit-men.

-Yes.

-At what point in the past do we arrive?

-May 26, 1947...precisely three years ago from tomorrow. But, you must act quickly. You will have only a matter of twenty-four hours to complete your assignment: from sunrise to sunrise and no more. It is critical that you remember this..

-And, just supposing I run into myself when I arrive. Does that trigger an explosion or something even worse? You see, I'm up on my science fiction.

Edward couldn't help but laugh at his own question.

-You will not meet your past self. It will be like two magnets repelling one another. The Edward Mendez of 1947 will sense your presence and instinctively keep his distance.

-How do we travel back? You got a time machine handy? You a friend of H.G. Wells'?

-You will be your own time mechanism...no other mechanism will be needed.

Edward put out his cigarette almost smashing it into the ashtray.

-How?

-This building was chosen for its structural form and location. On the roof just above us the triangle will merge into the mode of physical transportation. The focal point will be your mind's eye. You will travel along the grid network...the line that will send you back to the recent past. It will be like walking on a tightrope that one cannot fall off. The universe is composed of a grid work of intersecting lines...if one can see them, one can utilize them to his advantage.

-How do we know when to get off?

-Focus on your destination's date and time. You will know when to "step off."

-How do we see these "lines?"

-I will help you.

-And, just how do we get back?

-You and the Lieutenant will come back to this building. Experience will show you how to reverse the process.

-And, all of history is changed...and maybe for the worst.

-No, Edward. I've told you, only that "segment" is changed, but not in your mind or Donovan's. Your conscious recollection of things past and "undone" will remain lodged in your memory. It will be like correcting a mistake on a written exam. You erase the error and replace it with the correct answer. But, you don't forget the original answer even though it's been erased from sight.

Edward got up and walked the short distance to the door. He turned around to face his father.

-Who are the people you want us to kill?

-Mr. Heinrich Weiss, engineer. Karl Fassbinder, engineer. And, Miss Lisa Pabst, physicist. Two Germans and one American traitor. The woman is a traitor to her country of the United States.

-Where are they holed up.

-That I am unable to tell you. You must use your shamus skills and Lt. Donovan's police tactics.

Edward leaned against the door. His P. I. gut instinct was starting to kick in.

-I think I might know where to start.

-Excellent!

-And, this *will* work?

-It should.

-I don't like that answer. And, I don't like disrupting history. Don't ask me why, but I've got a bad feeling about this. It's like playing with a lit stick of dynamite.

Manuel Mendez ignored his son's concerns. There were no room for "concerns" at this point.

-You haven't objected to being an assassin. Good. Think of the lives you will be saving in that parallel universe, as well...millions, Edward. Not to mention the over three billion lives in this one. So, give me your answer or I'll be forced to engage someone else.

-Like whom?

-Myself. Your father. And, my age could impede both me and the mission.

-Where can I reach you? You'll know my answer by tonight.

-At Miranda Drake's home.

-I've got the number. And, right now, I'm working on another case.

-Lorraine Keyes's murder. It can wait. I read the papers. Interesting case, though, and maybe more complex than you might think.

-Talk to you tonight.

Edward opened the door to leave.

-Wait a moment, Edward, please. I have more to tell you.

Edward stood by the door waiting for his father to continue.

-So, tell me.

-A third assassin will be accompanying you and Lt. Donovan into the recent past: Mr. Roger Lee.

Edward pounded one fist into the other.

-I knew you were holding out. You want me to work with a hood? He's wanted for kidnapping and a few other charges.

-Mr. Roger Lee is as ruthless as they come. And, he knows the city like the back of his hand. He'll help guarantee success. I know...he's a felon and not to be trusted. But, to save his own neck, he'll do anything. One assassin for each of the three individuals.

-It goes against my better judgment.

-I'm aware of that. But, suspend your moral judgment for the sake of the world. One cannot always chose one's allies. Russia was once a trusted ally, at least during the latter part of the war.

-I hope you're not comparing Roger Lee to Stalin.

-No...but there are parallels.

Manuel Mendez took a deep breath.

-I've already spoken to Lt. Donovan. He is willing.

Edward grinned at his father.

-Does he know about our traveling companion?

-No. I'll leave that bit of news in your capable hands.

-Thanks...for nothing.

-Anyway, I shall hear from you tonight?

-No. I'll be here tomorrow. Count on it.

-Goodbye, Edward.

-Goodbye, father.

THREE

EDWARD TOOK the elevator down, not bothering to wait for his father. He assumed that his father was not yet ready to leave. The P. I. really didn't care. The descent was quicker than the ascent had been. This time, even the elevator operator smiled and was friendly. He was relaxed and so was the P. I.

When leaving the elevator, Edward waved goodbye. He was relieved and he didn't know why. He walked along the marble floor of the Flatiron Building, not sure if he should take the antiquated elevator right back up to the 22nd floor. A lot of questions were running through his head: how did his father know the identities of the targeted men and woman? How did he know of time travel? And did he know something about Lorraine Keyes? Edward had the feeling that he did.

The P. I. got into his DeSoto and drove down to Sullivan St. He wanted to do some first hand investigating. At the first red light, he lit up and took a deep drag on his cigarette. Man that tasted good. He flicked some cigarette ash into the car's ashtray and drove on.

He drove past Lorraine Keyes's address on Sullivan St. From the outside, everything looked normal except that the four metal garbage cans were missing. Probably being examined by the forensics at the 6th Precinct. Ya' never know what you might find in a garbage can.

Edward made a complete circuit around the block and then pulled up in front of Miss Keyes's former address. Luck was with him. The landlady, Mabel, was just coming out of the building holding a broom in one hand and a dust pan in the other. She stopped short and shrugged her shoulders. She was about to turn around and go back in when Edward called out to her from his DeSoto.

-Hey, Mabel! It's Edward Mendez. Hold up a second, will you?

She did more than that. She walked over to Edward's double parked car.

-Hello, Mr. Mendez. I guess I know why you're here. It's about poor Lorraine, isn't it?

-Is there a parking space I can use?

Mabel looked up and down the street to make sure that there was no traffic..

-Don't see any. But, you're okay for now. It's a quiet street, never that much traffic.

-Mabel? Tell me about Lorraine.

-Nice girl. Pretty much kept to herself. I really didn't know her that well.

-How long was she living here, Mabel?

-The day after the sun re-appeared in the sky. I was so happy that day. I think we all were.

-I'll say! But, about Lorraine, did she have many friends?

-No girlfriends. At least, I never saw any.

-Boyfriends?

-A few, but nothing serious as far as I could tell.

-How would you know?

-I'd see them once and never again. Mr. Mendez, I don't like to speak ill of the dead.

-It could help jail her murderer.

Mabel looked up and down the street, again, with a stern expression on her face.

-Would it? Let's not be naive. We both know who killed her. I read the papers. I'm up on my current events. It was one of those hit-men from that awful company, Romo-Ark. I'm right, aren't I?

Edward lit another cigarette before answering.

-Looks like it. It's got all the earmarks of a hit job. But, Mabel, Romo-Ark is not invulnerable. Believe me, I know. They can and have been brought down.

Mabel, who had been looking up the street at nothing in particular, now turned to look the P. I. straight in the eye.

-Thanks to you, Mr. Mendez, and that Officer Morales. I know all about it.

-A lot of people were involved in that take down, Mabel. Now...why would Lorraine Keyes be killed? What was her story?

-I was only in her apartment once or twice. I guess I can admit it now, especially to you. Some magazines had arrived for her and I didn't want to leave them just lying about in the hallway. My cat likes to play with magazines and newspapers. So, I used my pass key and let myself in.

Edward blew some smoke into the cool air.

-Keep talking to me, Mabel.

-Well, the place was neat enough, but not a stick of furniture had been moved. It was a furnished apartment. No pictures on the wall, no knick-knacks...you know, girlish things...and her studying to be an interior decorator. Even the bathroom was bare...clean, mind you, but no feminine touches like what you'd expect of a young girl. And the medicine chest was bare, practically. Only rubbing alcohol and four bottles of it, too. What do you make of that, Mr. Mendez? Why all the alcohol?

But, before the P. I. could answer...

-And, the magazines, not the ones I brought, mind, but the ones on the coffee table...never been so much as opened once. I'd swear to that. And, all Lorraine ever had on her was that little shoulder bag of hers and never anything else. As a matter of fact, she must have had all her meals out. Never seen her do any grocery shopping except for cigarettes.

Mabel shook her head in bewilderment.

-The more I think about her, the strangeness just keeps growing. Stop me, Mr. Mendez, if I'm boring you.

-Anything but, Mabel. Her one-time boyfriends did any of them wear black suits?

-God, no! I would've noticed that right off. No. They all seemed normal enough, if you get my drift. Young, handsome men...you don't think...

-No. She was no prostitute.

Edward lit another cigarette.

-Where did she go to school for this interior decorating?

-Its' called the "Interior Decorators Institute." What else? It's on the upper east side. I think it's 55th St and Lexington Ave. The whole building is loaded with show rooms. Busy as a beehive most of the time...or so I've heard.

-Hey, Mabel? You think if I got out of my car and headed on upstairs, I could have a look at Lorraine's apartment?

-It's been taped off by the cops. And, there's a cop up there now. But, he might let you in. He seems nice enough.

-Watch my car for a couple of minutes?

-You bet. It's a beauty. And, I can tell the girls that I helped Edward Mendez on one of his cases..

Edward took the stairs two at a time. When he reached Lorraine Keyes's apartment, he was greeted by a young Police Officer.

-Sorry, buddy, but this pad's off limits. Did you know the chick who lived here?

Edward liked this young, brassy cop.

-Briefly. Here's my P. I. license.

The young Police Officer glanced at it.

-Come on in, Mr. Mendez. You know the drill probably better than me.

Edward crouched down under the police tape and entered Lorraine Keyes's apartment for the second time. He was struck by the disarray of furniture. Mind you, there wasn't much of it, but the love seat was overturned, the end table had been smashed and the coffee table was on its side. Magazines were strewn about the carpeted floor and the girl's armoir was open revealing the girl's wardrobe.

The P. I. walked over to the armoire and looked in. Black dresses of different styles and lengths...all black. On the bottom of the cabinet were high heels: leather, suede, spiked heels, stacked heels and even flats.

Officer Graham was looking over Edward's shoulder.

-She liked black, that for sure. Who can figure out a dame?

-Another dame.

Edward wished that Yolanda were here with him. She could shed some light on this pretty bleak wardrobe. Why the hell all black?

The P. I., careful not to touch anything, walked into the bathroom. Everything was white: the semi-gloss paint on the walls and ceiling, the white tiles on the floor and the porcelain bathtub and sink. He opened the medicine cabinet. All it contained was four bottles of rubbing alcohol and nothing else...no cosmetics, no feminine toiletries. He shut the cabinet door and was now staring at his own reflection in the mirror.

-Did she live here or did she just use this place for appearance sake? Nothing in this pad makes any sense. A guy would live like this...maybe, but not a pretty, young girl.

He walked back into the living room and stooped down to look at the magazines that were strewn about the floor. Had they ever been read by the murdered girl? He couldn't make out any folds or creases in the magazine...nothing. So, who was the girl who called herself Lorraine Keyes? Was that even her real name?

He straightened up and spoke to the young Police Officer.

-Any signs of theft, Officer? Any jewelry box that's been emptied?

Officer Graham shook his head in the negative.

-Nope. Not even a bobby pin.

Edward thought back to his encounter with the girl. Had she worn any jewelry? His answer came quicker than he expected. No. No necklace. No bracelet. No earrings.

-I'll be damned. So, where do I go from here?

That answer came just as quickly.

-To East 55th St. and that Interior Decorating building.

FOUR

THERE WAS a mob scene at the East 55th St. building: mostly women but a few men could also be spotted among the crowd. It was a friendly type of crowd...there was no shoving or excessive shouting...just people talking about their trade and exchanging some inside gossip. Everyone was well dressed and well groomed. The P. I. was impressed. I guess these interior decorators had to look as good as the interiors that they created. It made sense. His sister, Victoria, would love it here. Maybe, he'd even tell her about it.

Edward made his way through the lobby to the Information Desk. A very beautiful young woman was standing behind that particular counter. She had jet black, shoulder length hair, dark eyes and full lips. Her figure was model slim and she had the high cheekbones to match. She wore a navy blue dress that showed her figure in stylish taste.

-May I help you?

-I hope so. Could you tell me where I could find the Interior Decorating School? There is one here, isn't there?

The young lady looked a little puzzled at the P. I.'s query.

-I'm afraid there isn't. The building has only display and show rooms for the trade, you understand. We do have wholesale offices on some of the upper floors.

-But, no training centers for students or aspirants?

-No. They usually learn their trade at the university or a specialized trade school. I can give you a list of them, if you like.

Edward thought about it for a second. He could always pass it over to Dottie to check out.

-Sure. I'll take that list, Miss...

-Jamie. Jamie Anne Farley.

-You oughta' be a model, Jamie, or do some voice over work. Your look and tone are hypnotic.

-Thank you so much. Here's that list for you.

He took the list from the beautiful girl. She had lovely manicured hands adorned by a pink pearl ring on the middle finger.

-Jamie? I'm Edward Mendez. I'm a private investigator.

-I should have recognized you, Mr. Mendez.

-Edward, please.

-Edward. Are you investigating a case here in the building?

-Actually, two cases, but they may be connected. It's too early to tell.

-You saved all our lives, Edward. Thank you.

-You're welcome. And, I will return this list to you.

-Oh, Edward, you may keep it.

-It'll give me an excuse to see you again, Jamie.

-Should I play hard to get? I don't want to. I'd like to see you, again, Edward.

-Saturday, Jamie. How about a carriage ride through Central Park?

Jamie was flushed with pleasure.

-I'd love it. You can pick me up at my place on 59 Beach St. It's just off West St. It's actually within walking distance of your office.

-Saturday, 10 A.M. Bye, for now.

Edward folded the list and made to leave. For the moment, he was a happy man, trying to keep down his erection.

Marlena Lake, Susan Broder and Irene Wong were headed toward midtown in Marlena's car. Susan was driving and staying within the speed limit. Marlena and Irene were in the back seat discussing strategy.

-Miss Lake? Do you think that we'll be allowed into Dr. Lange's office? Miss Riley can be very difficult.

-I know. But, we'll get in...somehow. I really don't see how she can refuse us. Her life is at risk as much as anyone.

-Yes. But, will she see it that way? Her emotions may cloud her judgment. I believe that she was in love with Dr. Lange.

-How unfortunate for her.

-And, she never liked me. She only tolerated me because of my work with Dr. Lange.

-Don't over rate her importance, Miss Wong. She was a receptionist who thought a great of herself.

-But, we might need her cooperation.

-I don't think so.

Susan spoke up from the driver's seat while keeping her eyes on the road.

-We're almost there. And, mother, shouldn't we have waited for Lt. Donovan's subpoena to come through? I don't think he'd appreciate our going down there on our own.

-I've no patience with red tape. Can you find a parking space, dear? There doesn't seem to be any.

-Looking for one.

-Please, hurry, dear. I feel that time is against us.

It took Susan the better part of fifteen minutes to find a parking space. Finally, she found one and it was just up the block from Dr. Lange's office. The three women got out and walked the short distance. The guard let them in and they took the elevator up to the third floor office.

Mary Riley was not at her desk when they stepped out of the elevator...much to their relief.

-What a shame.

-Disappointed, mother?

Marlena ignored her daughter's slightly sarcastic remark.

-Well, ladies, let's stroll on in and see what we can uncover.

Marlena led the way to Dr. Lange's office at the end of the corridor. She did knock before entering and got no response. She opened the door and walked in. Irene and Susan followed.

The office was tidy enough. Dr. Lange's old desk was in the same place just opposite the window where the blinds were drawn and closed. Marlena turned on the lights.

-That's better. Look...there's the file cabinet.

-I will look through the files. I know what to look for.

-Mother, I don't feel quite right about this. We should have waited for that subpoena.

-Please, don't bore me with details. Dr. Lange owes it to humanity. Now, let's not waste any more time discussing it.

Marlena sat down at the desk. Susan knelt down and started going through the left hand set of drawers.

Each desk drawer was empty. Marlena's search of the right hand desk drawers brought the same result.

-This desk has been emptied out.

-Mother, check the middle drawer. Maybe there's something in there.

The middle desk drawer was empty...not so much as a paper clip was in it.

Marlena sat back in the desk chair and looked over to where Irene was standing. She called out to the Asian scientist.

-Oh, Miss Wong, any luck?

-The file cabinets are empty. That's very strange, but I found what I was looking for. It's my own journal with a few supplementary notes by Dr. Lange, himself.

Irene held up the book for the two women to see. Marlena was incredulous at the find.

-And, it was actually left behind? How in the world did Miss Riley miss it?

-It was hidden, Miss Lake. It was taped under the bottom file drawer.

-Well done, Miss Wong.

Susan spoke candidly to Irene.

-In a word or two, what's in it? How can it help us? What I'm trying to say is: what's the hurry? If the Earth is drifting slowly away from the sun, don't we have at least a little time to formulate a plan?

Miss Wong's expression was quite grim when she answered Susan.

Doomsday

-No, Miss Broder-

-Susan, please.

-I'm sorry, Susan. Doomsday may be only days away. I will explain. I should have done so before.

Irene took a deep breath before continuing.

-An asteroid the size of Australia is on a collision course with the Earth. If we do not correct the Earth's orbit, mankind will be wiped out. No one will survive such a collision.

FIVE

TRACY THIELEN met Officer Morgan Andes at the 86th Station House. Both she and her patrolman boyfriend were sitting in Lt. Donovan's office. Tracy and Lt. Donovan were smoking. Officer Andes was sipping a container of tepid black coffee.

Lt. Donovan started them off with a question.

-So, Tracy, your company at Thunder American knew about this for how long?

-I'm not too sure of the timeline, but I think it goes back to the sun's disappearance. Scientists around the world have been tracking the Earth's velocity and orbital path. They knew of the fluctuation in its orbit back then, but some thought it would either correct itself or stabilize in its new orbit. It hasn't.

-Which brings us to the present.

Tracy tried smiling, but couldn't quite manage it.

-Lieutenant? Morgan? We have less time than you think.

-Yes, Miss Thielen? More bad news?

-Yes. An asteroid that would have missed the Earth had it stayed on its original orbit, is hurtling directly on a collision course with us.

Lt. Donovan's fist slammed down on his desk.

-When, for God's sake? *When*?

-Days away. By this time tomorrow, it will be visible in the northern sky...maybe even sooner

Morgan finished his coffee and stared out the window at nothing in particular. What was there to see? What was the point? It would all be gone.

-Irene, what is in your journal? You must tell me.

-Of course, Miss Lake.

Susan was driving them back to her mother's townhouse. She also was dying of curiosity as to the journals contents.

-Contained within the journal are calculations on time and matter displacement.

-How does that help us? Mind you, I understand the theory and the task of transferring matter through time and space and even shifting time, but...the practical applications escape me. In short, how can theory save us?

-They may help Lt. Donovan and Edward. If what I suspect is true, they will be traveling back through the space-time continuum.

-Of course! The Flatiron Building...at dawn. I should have surmised as much. And, you had already surmised this for yourself, Miss Wong. You are not only intelligent, but keenly perceptive. And of course, I must be there tomorrow when the attempt is made. But, how in the world will it be done?

Irene answered Marlena's question as best she could..

-The tilt of the axis combined with the energy of its rotation will be the thrusting power...the lift-off, if you will.

-And, the act of transference..the initial act of transference?

-Literally, the conscious mind over matter. Consciousness, Marlena, where is it actually located? Do you know? Does anyone know? Is it in one's brain? Or on the ceiling? Is it hovering just above one's body? I suspect the latter.

Susan spoke...wanting to sort things out in her own head.

-So, the two men's consciousness will travel backward in time and not their actual bodies? Is that what you're telling us?

Irene now looked worried.

-I believe that Manuel Mendez will attempt a physical transference. And, that might prove fatal to both men. The mind is much more malleable than the physical body. The mind could enter the bodies of Edward and Lt. Donovan unscathed. Hopefully, that will be the object of Manuel Mendez's attempt.

Irene turned to face Marlena. She was worried.

-But, can this man be trusted?

-Do you trust him, Miss Wong? What does your woman's intuition tell you?

-No. I don't trust him.

-Neither do I. He is a man with many hidden motives.

Edward Mendez, P. I. was standing on the roof of his mother's house in Brooklyn Heights. He'd just lit a fresh cigarette and was walking the length of the rooftop. It was dusk and he had his blazer on to keep out the chill of the approaching evening. He should have been thinking about tomorrow...about his "meeting" atop the Flatiron Building with his father and the Lieutenant and Roger Lee. He wasn't. His mind was on the young woman he'd met today: Jamie Anne Farley. There was something so intimately familiar about the girl...but what was it? He'd been drawn to her...to her quiet but confident manner...by the way she comported herself...and by her classic beauty. Her scent still remained with him like a cool, ocean breeze that arouses the senses...a man's senses.

He flicked the ash from his cigarette and stopped walking. He had to travel back in time three years...not so very long ago. If he and Lt. Donovan were successful, how much of history would actually be changed? Only the events along that "grid line" of time...or so his father assumed. But, how could Manuel Mendez know that for certain? He couldn't. He was guessing.

Edward shook his head and tossed his cigarette butt to the floor and stomped on it. He went back downstairs to the family living room. He took out his notepad and dialed Jamie's number. She picked up on the second ring.

-Hello?

-Jamie? It's Edward Mendez.

-I was about to call you, Edward. I have so much to say, but I don't know just how to say it.

-It's funny, but I think I know what you mean. Do you have the feeling, Jamie, that we've known each other...or at least have met before today?

-Yes! That's exactly how I feel. And, not just in casual passing. It's much more than that. I can't explain it.

-Me neither. Saturday, Jamie...

-No Edward. Let's meet tomorrow. I can't wait until Saturday. It's too far off.

-That won't be easy. It will have to be early morning.

-I don't care how early it is. Please.

-The Flatiron Building, do you know where it is?

-Yes. I've been there.

-If I'm not waiting for you in the lobby, come to the top floor, the corner office at the point of the building.

-I'll be there. What time, Edward?

-Say a little before 6 o'clock? Too early?

-I'll be there. Promise.

-And, Jamie?

-Yes?

-I can't promise you Saturday. I might not...

-What? What is it, Edward? Are you going on an assignment...a dangerous assignment?

-It could be dangerous. But, I have to go.

-And, you might not come back, is that what you're trying to tell me? Because I won't accept that. You will come back and I'll be waiting for you.

-You're giving me just what I need, Jamie. Now, I think I *can* succeed. Thanks. And, listen, take a cab tomorrow to the Flatiron Building. Don't use public transportation.

-I will.

-Now, get some rest.

They ended the call. Edward went into the kitchen for some much needed black coffee and a smoke.

Nathalie Montaigne was having a restless night. She turned over in her bed and grabbed at the alarm clock on the night table.

-Mon Dieu! Only 11 o'clock. I must get up and read for awhile. Perhaps, that will induce sleep or at least pass the time.

Nathalie got out of bed and put on her robe and satin slippers. She went into the bathroom to wash her hands, not daring to look at her reflection in the cabinet mirror.

-Why upset myself?

She knew that her hair was far too long for her age. She planned to get it cut and coiffed tomorrow if time permitted. Perhaps, that would help, although she doubted it. But, at least, she could put a comb through the salt-and-pepper mess.

She walked back into the small living room and picked up a paperback novel in French. It was Simenon's latest effort; an author who she greatly admired for his direct prose and quite interesting plots. She opened the book and was about to sit down when she heard a woman's scream. She dropped the novel on to the sofa and for a moment sat perfectly still. Was someone being assaulted or robbed? In a big city like New York, it was always a distinct possibility.

Nathalie once again picked up her novel. And, then, another scream pierced the night air causing her to drop her book to the floor.

-But, that was someone quite different. Mon Dieu, but what is going on out there?

Nathalie went over to the window. She opened it and looked out. There were a few pedestrians on the sidewalk, but nothing untoward seemed to be occurring in the street below. She did notice that most of the pedestrians had stopped and were looking skyward. What in the world were they staring at so intently?

Doomsday

Nathalie leaned further out the window and looked skyward, but saw nothing but the night sky overhead.

The Frenchwoman called down to anyone who would listen.

-But, what is happening? Please, someone tell me.

A man looked up in Nathalie's direction. He pointed skyward, but didn't say anything.

Nathalie shifted her position and saw it: a bright, red dot in the night sky and it was not the planet, Mars. No. She knew this and almost screamed in terror.

-An asteroid! How terrifying.

The man staring up at Nathalie shouted.

-The end of the world, lady! Judgment day is upon us! Confess your sins...if it'll do any damned good.

Nathalie pulled herself back in and collapsed on to the sofa, but not before another woman screamed into the night.

Part III
Doomsday

ONE

THE NEWS bulletin was broadcast that Friday morning. People were already hazarding guesses as to the bright, red dot moving across the sky.

-It can't be Mars. No way.

-It's too damned bright and it's moving too fast.

-And, too damned close.

-My God! I'll bet it's a meteor and it's coming straight at us.

-Will it hit the Earth? And, how big is it?

-Maybe, it'll burn up in the atmosphere.

-What the hell is the government doing about it? That's what I want to know.

-What do they ever do about anything? Nothing!

-It could be nothing.

-You hope.

Doomsday

Edward Mendez was with Jamie in the lobby of the Flatiron Building when the official broadcast came over the air waves at 5:30 A.M. The night watchman was still on duty. He had his portable radio turned up. The three people listened.

"At 10 P.M. E.S.T. last night a celestial object appeared over the northern hemisphere. It is an asteroid that orbits the sun in much the same manner as the Earth. Its orbit is an elongated ellipse and it is now approaching the Earth. The chances are that it will either graze the Earth's atmosphere or strike our planet within the next forty-eight hours. The military has taken steps to avoid such a collision and, at the same time, correct the Earth's own orbit around the sun. The Earth has drifted from its original orbit because of the disappearance of the sun two and a half years ago.

"As we speak, atomic devices are being placed in the Aleutian Islands which is right off the territory of Alaska and also near the continent of Antarctica.

"We are not alone in this undertaking. Russia and Great Britain have joined us in this effort to save the world. Scientists from around the globe have contributed and all agree that action must be taken and soon.

"We will not downplay the danger. But, to do nothing would indeed be fatal even if the asteroid were not to strike the Earth. The government has asked that everyone go about their business as usual. However, we urge you to stay close to your homes. Further instructions will be forthcoming on an hourly basis."

The jazz music came back on. The night watchman grunted in disgust and picked up his newspaper.

-Jamie, let's head on up. We don't have too much time.

The night watchman looked up from his paper as Edward and Jamie approached him.

-Elevator operator's not on duty yet. You know how to work that vertical contraption?

-I think so. Do you mind if I give it a try? You won't get into trouble, will you?

-Me? Hell, no. Didn't you just hear that fool announcer on the radio. It's the end of the damned world. That rock in the sky is either gonna' pulverize us or we're gonna' blow ourselves to Kingdom come!

Jamie touched the old man's arm.

-I think we're going to come through this.

-Hope you're right, young lady. You and your boyfriend can head on up any time you like.

Jamie smiled at the gruff but kind man.

-Thank you.

Edward stepped into the elevator and Jamie followed him in.

-Here goes nothing. Hold on, baby.

-Take it slow, Edward, until you get the hang of it.

The P. I. did just that. He closed the steel accordion door and pushed down gently on the vertical lever. Slowly, the two people ascended the skyscraper.

-I think I'll try just a little more pressure.

-Careful, Edward.

The elevator car sped up. And, in a matter of less than a minute, they were on the 22nd floor.

Jamie put her arm through Edward's and smiled up at him.

-You're a talented man.

-You're welcome. Here's the office. Let's go on in.

The small office was empty. The sun's morning glow was just visible over the horizon. The air was chilly but pleasant.

Edward? Why are we here in this place?

-It's where my assignment begins, Jamie.

She looked about the small office.

-Here? I don't understand.

-I'm going back in time to change the course of history...to make sure that all of this never happens. It's the only way considering the alternative.

-Edward...it's insane, but I'm beginning to understand. How will you do it...go back in time?

The P. I. smiled and looked into Jamie's dark, brown eyes.

-I don't know, but my father, Manuel Mendez, does. He's an occultist. You might as well know who you're getting mixed up with, Jamie. Have I scared you off yet?

-No. But, Edward, will I see you, again? And, if I do, will we know each other?

-Yes. Didn't you say that you felt you already knew me?

-I did. And, I still feel that way.

-So do I.

-I'm afraid, Edward...afraid that something terrible will happen to you.

-Nothing's gonna' happen to me.

He reached into his jacket pocket. The suit he had on was a new one: a soft, cotton gray that would help the P. I. blend in with the crowds of Manhattan. He would be a businessman wearing his two piece suit with matching Fedora.

-Here.

He handed Jamie a fresh pack of cigarettes.

-Keep this for me. And, here are the matches.

Jamie took the pack of Lucky Strike from Edward.

-I'll take good care of this. We'll share a smoke when you get back.

-When I come back to you. If I had a ring, I'd give it to you, Jamie.

-This is just fine. Anything of yours would be fine.

Edward looked at his wristwatch.

-The others should be here soon.

As the P. I. spoke those words, the office door opened and Manuel Mendez walked in.

Marlena Lake had been up for hours. Where was Edward Mendez...at the Flatiron Building...and why hadn't he called her? What was he up to? She had to know for certain and quickly. She'd heard the news bulletin on the radio. They now had less than forty-eight hours before the detonations. Susan had come down earlier. Marlena had ordered her daughter back upstairs to awaken Miss Wong. Information is what Marlena demanded as she paced the floor of her study. She was already dressed to go out. Her handbag was on the coffee table in the living room.

Of course...Edward's sister, Dottie, would know of her brother's whereabouts.

Marlena dialed Edward's business number. It wasn't yet six o'clock, but the P. I. might be in. He didn't keep regular hours. And, she would not hang up until someone answered. Dottie Mendez picked up.

-Hello?

-Dottie? It's Marlena Lake. Where is Edward? I simply must know.

Dottie thought that this woman doesn't beat about the bush.

-He's at the Flatiron Building on 22nd St.

-I know where it is...and what is he doing there. Has he confided in you?

-You know? I'm not supposed to know...

-But, you do, Miss Mendez.

-Eddie's meeting with our father on some kind of wild...trip? A trip through time.

-Then, Miss Wong and I were correct in our assumptions. Your brother is attempting to alter that thread of history. It may be our only salvation.

-Marlena? You better hurry if you want to catch up with my intrepid brother. I think lift-off is close to the sun coming over the horizon...but I could be wrong. It's the only reason I'm here so damned early in the morning.

-Yes. Yes. The timing of such an attempt would be critical. Thank you, my dear. I must run.

-Oh, Marlena, be careful. I hear that in certain parts of the city, riots are breaking out. Panic's setting in...for all the good it will do.

-What did those fools expect? They should never have made that announcement. Goodbye and stay safe.

Marlena hung up and raced halfway up the stairs. She shouted out to her daughter.

-Susan! Come here quickly and bring Miss Wong with you. Hurry! You're both taking too long.

That last word came out rather like a shrill. Susan rushed to the head of the staircase. She knew that when her mother was in a panic, the situation had to be dire. Miss Wong came out of her bedroom still putting on her pink bathrobe.

Doomsday

-Mother, what in the world is it?

-Get dressed. Quickly! Don't bother with the amenities of primping...simply get dressed and get the car ready. We're going downtown. Within fifteen minutes, we must be on our way or it will be too late.

Susan turned about and headed back to her room as ordered. She motioned for Miss Wong to do the same.

Marlena went back downstairs and grabbed her handbag off the coffee table. She checked its contents making certain that her gun was loaded. She paced the living room floor waiting for the two girls to come down. And, her active mind was full of varying thoughts.

-Did Miss Wong know about the planned detonations scheduled for tomorrow? And, why had she not confided this information to her? She must question the girl at length.

Marlena walked to the foot of the staircase. She was about to call out, again, when Susan came running down the stairs flinging her shoulder bag on. Miss Wong was not far behind wearing her usual Mandarin style dress. She carried only a small purse with her. She had not bothered to apply any make-up. Why bother when the world was about to come to an end?

-Fast enough for you, mother?

-Good girl. We must hurry.

She turned her attention to Irene.

-Miss Wong, are you all set?

-I think so. But, where are we going so early in the morning? The sun hasn't even risen.

-To the Flatiron Building to save this damned world of ours.

-Then, it's to be today. It is frightening.

-Yes, it is. Susan bring the car around front. I'll lock up.

Susan did as she was told. Marlena turned back to Miss Wong.

-Did you know that they planned to detonate those warhead late tomorrow?

Irene was taken aback by this not-so-veiled accusation.

-No. I swear that I didn't. Why do you ask?

-That asteroid that you told us about...it's about to collide with the Earth.

-My God! The moon's gravitational pull must have put it on a direct collision course with the Earth. This is terrible news.

Marlena grinned.

-You have a flair for the understatement. It seems that we're surrounded by a series of cataclysms.

-It does seem... I don't want to say it.

-Is "hopeless" the word you're groping for, Miss Wong?

A car's horn sounded outside.

Doomsday

-That must be Susan. Come. We've no time to waste.

TWO

RIOTING WAS quickly becoming rampant throughout New York City and other cities around the world. People across the globe were panicking...screaming in desperation at a situation that they felt was hopeless.

-Stay calm, they tell us. Bloody easy for them safely tucked away only God knows where.

-They're gonna' save the planet by blowing it up? It's lunacy. They'll kill us all.

-Can't they send a missile up there to blow the thing out of the sky? They know how to blow up cities.

-And, people in them! *That* they can do.

-What about the fall-out? If the asteroid doesn't do us in, the radiation will.

-I'm staying home. I'll die with my family, I will.

-Why are these idiots thinking that's gonna' help? What's the point? We'll all be dead by tomorrow, anyway.

Doomsday

Morgan Andes and Tracy Thielen arrived at the Flatiron Building a few minutes after Edward's arrival. Morgan parked just across the street from the 23rd St. park. People were gathering and talking, but there was no sign of violence...not yet.

-Let's head on in, Tracy. It's peaceful over there for now. But, who knows for how long.

-I'm with you, Morgan.

They ran across the street and into the building. Morgan knew the night watchman on duty. He gave them the go ahead to head on up, telling them that another couple had just gone up. They stepped into the elevator.

-Morgan, do you know how to operate this thing?

-Just watch me. My father handled one of these for a time.

He closed the two gates and upwards they zoomed. On the 22nd floor...

-Morgan, I'm impressed. And, my stomach is still where it should be.

Morgan laughed as he took Tracy's hand and led her out of the elevator..

-Glad to hear it. Let's head on up to the roof, shall we?

-That's why we're here, isn't it?

The two people walked to the exit and climbed the staircase leading up to the roof.

-Morgan, wait a minute.

-What is it? I know you're not afraid of heights.

-I'm afraid of what we'll find out there. I have a terrible feeling about all this.

-It's this or we're finished, Tracy. Edward gave me the low down last night.

-I know. You're right. Of course, you're right.

-Come on. I won't let you out of my sight.

-You better not.

Morgan opened the roof door. They stepped out into the open air and were met by a strong gust of wind. Tracy noticed the stillness in the air despite the initial gust of wind She and Morgan walked over to the rooftop's edge and waited for the others to arrive.

Ginny Gray's by-line was complete. It was a real "winner" of a headline.

"No Way Out?"

She had to put the question mark there to give at least some shred of hope to her readers. But...was there any hope?

Ginny sat at her desk pondering who to call first. Edward Mendez won. She dialed his home number. Nella Mendez picked up.

-Mendez residence.

-It's Ginny Gray. Where the hell is Edward?

-And, good morning to you, Miss Gray. Well..if my sister Dottie is to be relied upon, he's at the Flatiron Building as we speak.

-Why so damned early?

-My brother and father are attempting to save the world. And, it won't be for the first time.

Ginny laughed out loud into the receiver.

-I should have guessed! Nella...this is Nella?

-It is.

-Sorry to be so brusque, but time's running out and fast. I must run. Oh! And, Nella, stay indoors. Things are getting heated in the city.

-And, you be careful, Ginny. I'll pray for you all.

-Do that, baby! We need all the help we can get.

Ginny grabbed her shoulder bag and sweater and quite literally raced out of the press room.

Susan pulled up to the Flatiron Building, but there were no parking spaces available.

-There! Susan, just park the car in front of the main entrance. We can't waste time looking for a parking space.

-Well, it should be all right. It doesn't say that I *can't* park there.

Susan maneuvered the car into the "right" place like a pro. The three women piled out of the car. The young woman looked up at the skyscraper.

-Where in the building, mother?

-My guess is the roof. Quickly! The sun is about to rise.

The three women rode up in the elevator with Susan operating the controls. They arrived safely on the 22nd floor.

-Well done.

Miss Wong agreed with beaming admiration.

-You did that very well, Susan. You're very adept.

Susan let out a sigh of relief.

-Thank you. I can start breathing, again.

At the far end of the corridor, Edward, Jamie and his father came out of the small office at the "point." The two men and Jamie approached the three women. Edward was the first to speak.

-Marlena, your timing is damned perfect.

-Of course, dear boy. Now, what is our next move?

Manuel Mendez answered her question.

-We go on up to the roof, Miss Lake.

-Go on, please.

-And, form the triangle of manifestation.

-I don't follow you, Mr. Mendez. What exactly are we to "manifest?"

-A timeline to the past...a grid line...one of the many that holds the universe together. Edward and Lt. Donovan will follow it to their destination.

Susan broke in with a question of her own.

-Why Lt. Donovan, Mr. Mendez?

-Because he is ruthless and has both military and police training.

Susan continued to question Mr. Mendez.

-But, why not Officer Andes, as well?

-I have my reasons. Officer Andes will be our guard on the roof...our "black guardian," if you will. There is rioting in the streets below. We may need his protection.

The elevator door opened and Ginny Gray stepped out.

-It looks like I'm not too late for the party. It's starting to get real ugly out there. You can't go near Times Square. The mob has stopped all traffic.

Manuel Mendez gave his order.

-Come. We're wasting time. Edward, lead the way, please.

Everyone followed the P. I. on to the roof. What they didn't see was the figure of Mr. Roger Lee following at a safe distance behind. He'd been hiding in one of the side offices, waiting for Manuel Mendez's signal to come out. He spotted Irene. She hadn't spoken a word. Well, she was always on the quiet side. Maybe...just maybe...if the opportunity presented itself, Roger Lee would throw her off the rooftop...even if it meant upsetting Mendez's plan. But, for now, he'd keep quiet and not step on to the rooftop proper...not until he got the signal.

Morgan and Tracy were already on the roof. They had been looking at the gathering crowd across the street in the park. It was starting to become unruly and loud. The two people were standing across from the rooftop door. They were waiting for someone...anyone...to arrive. Edward was the first person to emerge on to the rooftop.

Morgan put his arm about Tracy's waist.

-Hey, Tracy, there's my buddy, Eddie, and his new girlfriend. He doesn't let the grass grow under him. I'll introduce you. You okay, baby? You look kinda' scared.

-I'll be fine.

He kissed Tracy lightly on the lips and made way for the others to come out on to the roof.

Edward and Jamie walked over to the couple.

-Morgan? Tracy? Glad you could make it. I'd like you to meet Jamie Farley.

Introductions were made, but Morgan got straight to the point.

-So, Eddie, what's going on? What's expected of me?

Edward grinned at his friend's very good question.

-You're gonna' be the "rear" guard, pal. We need you to protect the troops.. And, time's running out real fast. Maybe, we oughta' call this a suicide mission.

-But, what the hell is the mission? I know you told me, but...

-Time travel, Morgan. Don't you keep up on current events?

And, on another part of the roof, Manuel Mendez and company had gathered. Ginny Gray was trying to pry some information out of the P. I.'s enigmatic father.

-Well, Mr. Mendez, are we up here to save mankind or wave to the mob below?

-My hope is to save mankind, Miss Gray. We both want to live, no?

-I won't even answer that one. So, how are we gonna' do it?

-Miss Gray?

-Just how do you propose to save us?

-Through the science of the ancients and quantum mechanics.

Irene Wong was standing with her back to the door. She thought that she heard a movement behind her on the stairwell. She turned around. Was that the figure of a man hidden in the darkness? It was. And, she thought that she recognized the man...Roger Lee!

Irene grabbed a hold of the door and slammed it shut. Everyone on the roof turned to look at her. Marlena asked Miss Wong what the matter was.

-Miss Wong, whatever is wrong?

-Roger Lee is down there. I just saw him on the stairwell.

Manuel Mendez stepped forward and took a hold of the door's handle.

-Mr. Lee is here by my leave. We will need his criminal instincts and underground contacts if we're to be successful.

Someone was now climbing the stairs and it was more than one person. There was a loud knock from inside. Manuel Mendez opened the door and out stepped Roger Lee with his hands in the air followed by Lt. Donovan. Both men were sporting business suits that would blend in with the crowd, similar to what Edward was affecting..

Roger Lee turned on Manuel Mendez. His face was red with fury.

-You set me up...double-crossing bastard!

Manuel Mendez raised a placating hand.

-No. The timing was off, that is all. You were not sent here to be arrested.

Lt. Donovan, who was still holding his gun to the back of Roger Lee, calmly stated.

-He's under arrest as of now.

-No, Lieutenant. We need his skill. Trust me. To save his own neck, Mr. Lee will do anything that I ask of him.

Irene spoke up and contradicted that last statement.

-Don't count on that. If you do, then you are a fool. Roger is cunning and treacherous and listens to no one but himself.

-Shut your mouth, you bitch!

Annoyed, Marlena pointed toward the eastern sky.

-Everyone...look to the east. The sun is about to rise.

Manuel Mendez now took charge.

-Then, we must begin.

-Without Mr. Lee, here, Mr. Mendez.

-Lieutenant, please. I beg of you. Trust me to save the world. Mr. Lee knows what is expected of him.

Manuel Mendez turned to Roger Lee.

-Tell the Lieutenant, Mr. Lee.

-I know what to do. And, in exchange for my help, I go free.

Lt. Donovan was about to speak, but Manuel Mendez cut him off.

-A small price to pay for billions of lives, wouldn't you say, Lieutenant?

For a moment, Lt. Donovan thought it over.

-You win. But, this boy's carrying a rod.

-He won't dare use it.

Manuel Mendez turned to the others on the roof.

-Now, everyone, with the exception of myself, Roger Lee and Edward, will leave the rooftop and wait on the floor below. Please, hurry. The sun is almost in direct alignment with the "point" of this rather unusual skyscraper.

Reluctantly, everyone made for the stairwell. Marlena was the last to go. She gave Edward a meaningful look that said.

-Don't trust Roger Lee or your father.

When they reached the bottom of the stairwell, Morgan advised them all to move one more flight down.

-I don't know how they're going back in time, but I think we oughta' put another floor between us and them.

Marlena agreed with the Police Officer.

-Officer Andes is quite right. The energy that Manuel Mendez is unleashing could be dangerous.

Morgan led the way down the next flight of stairs. Without anyone noticing, Irene was the last to follow. She held back deliberately. Taking off her high heels, she tiptoed back up to the rooftop carrying her shoes in one hand. She was a scientist and had to see for herself the mechanism of time travel. It was science not yet explained and not the nonsense of magic. What else could it be? However, to bend the so-called laws of physics...she must be a witness to such an event.

Meanwhile on the rooftop...

-Gentlemen? Look straight ahead and at nothing else. Focus on the horizon that you cannot see.

Edward and Lt. Donovan found it difficult not to look at Manuel Mendez. Roger Lee was blinded by the sun's light. He didn't see Irene sneaking back on to the roof and neither did anyone else.

Manuel Mendez continued to speak and give instructions.

Doomsday

-The grid is beneath your feet, gentlemen. Step on it even though you cannot yet see it. Do not even attempt to look at it at this particular point in time. Feel its non-weight. Your three paths will crisscross, but you will meet at the crossroads of infinity that will bring you back to the recent past. And, one last thing: you may have only twenty-four hours before you are "pulled" back to this time. I am not certain of the time frame, but...do not trifle with it.

Irene was standing behind Edward and still the P. I. did not see the Asian scientist. His peripheral vision was gone. And, yes...he was hovering a few inches off the tarmac. He began to move as if propelled along a moving sidewalk...and yet he walked as if in a trance...a trance of his own making.

The three men moved toward and, then, through each other until each went past the edge of the roof and vanished from sight.

Manuel Mendez pointed to Miss Wong.

-Step on the grid line, young lady. Follow my son. He'll need your cunning and scientific knowledge.

Irene placed herself where Edward had been standing.

-Focus, Miss Wong on May 27, 1947...and walk forward. Now.

Irene's feet were touching something that held no danger and, yet, the slightest wavering of thought would mean her death.

Manuel Mendez put away the Sumerian amulet that he'd been holding. In fact, it was a device...an ancient device that triggered the speed of thought within a person's mind. It was a technology that was lost to modern man..a technology brought to Earth millennia ago by the Anunanki...the people of the forgotten planet.

Meanwhile on the 21st floor, Irene Wong's absence had been noticed. Susan was the first one to exclaim-

-Where's Irene? She did come down with us, didn't she?

Jamie, looking about the corridor, replied.

-I didn't notice her, Miss Broder. Could she be in the restroom?

-I'll look.

Susan looked in the 21st floor restroom, but it was empty. She came out and shook her head.

-Not in there. I'll check upstairs.

-I'll go with you, my dear. But, I strongly suspect that the enigmatic Miss Wong went back up to the roof to join the men.

-Mother, you're not serious.

-Quite serious. Come, let's make certain.

Morgan spoke to the group at large.

-Maybe, we'd better all go back up.

Ginny Gray was annoyed with herself.

-Damn it! I should have thought to go back up. That little bitch beat me to it. Well, just maybe, I can make up for lost time.

The reporter followed the others back up to the 22nd floor. But, as Susan and Marlena went to check the ladies restroom and the others were looking through each office, opening doors and peering in, Ginny ran up the stairwell that led to the rooftop. She flung open the iron door to be confronted by Manuel Mendez.

-Too late, Miss Gray. They've gone.

-And, Miss Wong? Was she too late?

-No. But, you must not stay here. I must take up the vigil...a brief one to be sure. They will be back at any moment.

Ginny Gray looked at this man with incredulous eyes.

-What the hell are you saying?

-You must leave, Miss Gray. The grid must not be disrupted.

Ginny Gray was furious at herself and Manuel Mendez.

-And, Irene Wong was the exception? What made her so special?

-Yes and no. I remembered that she had been...there.

-You "remembered?" What the hell does that mean?

-Yes. Now, please, go back down with the others. You won't have long to wait.

He stepped forward and slammed the door in Ginny Gray's face.

.

Part IV
The Assassins

ONE

EDWARD FELL on to a seat in a moving subway car. Miss Irene Wong fell into his lap. Both people were momentarily stunned and disoriented. Their vision was blurred, but quickly came back into focus. The few passengers riding in that particular subway car turned to look in their direction. Where had these two people come from? And why such an exhibition of affection?

Edward held on to Miss Wong who placed her arm about his shoulder. The P. I. didn't seem too surprised by the young woman's presence. He looked around to get his bearings. What train were they on and in what direction were they headed? And, where were Lt. William Donovan and Roger Lee? How would he and Irene find them if they weren't riding the same train as they? And, the most important question of all: had they succeeded in reaching the year 1947?

First things first. He eased Irene off his lap and gently sat her next to him on the hard, straw seat. Her arm was still about his shoulder.

-Irene? You tagging along on this ride?

-Yes. I hope that you don't mind the company. Do you, Edward?

-No. But, I better get up and see where we're headed.

-Edward, the others...where are they? I don't see them. Did they make it through?

Edward stood up and "shook" the goosebumps off.

-I'll look around. You stay put for now.

-Okay.

Edward was about to approach a young man to ask for directions, but the train pulling into the 28th St. stop saved him the trouble. He turned back to Irene.

-Irene, we're getting off here. Let's go.

She got up clutching her handbag and joined Edward at the door.

-The train's heading uptown. We must have been catapulted right around 23rd St. which makes sense, in a way – sort of a sling shot effect.

-We're coming to a stop. Maybe, the others will get off too. Maybe, they're riding in a different car on this same train.

-If they're not, our rendezvous point was the Flatiron Building or at least it should have been. Time's not on or side. My father said that even though we traveled through the time barrier, we're still tethered to our point of departure. In fact, we're still "walking" on the grid line.

-Yes. That would make sense. We really don't belong here and time and nature have a "habit" of correcting themselves.

-Here's our stop.

Edward and Irene stepped off the uptown local train and on to the subway platform. It took Edward a second to orient himself in the proper direction. He took Irene by the hand and led her toward the exit. A few other passengers had gotten off and were headed to the uptown exit. The air felt fresh and warm as the train pulled out. Irene's high heels made clicking noises on the concrete floor. Edward liked that sound...so feminine and sensual.

The two people emerged from the subway and found themselves on 28th and Broadway.

-I just can't see taking the train back for one lousy stop.

-I don't mind walking.

-Irene, can you feel that breeze?

-Yes. Why do you ask?

-Feel it. *Really* feel it. It's warm. It's a warm breeze with no chill to it. Irene, it's *warm*!

Edward stopped in his tracks. Yes. Irene knew now what the P. I. meant. The warm breeze blew her long hair about and...it felt wonderful and comforting.

-Edward, it must be 1947 or at least a time prior to the sun's disappearance. The air is free of that terrible chill.

The P. I. was breathing in the warm and intoxicating air.

-You bet. Look. There's a cop just on the corner.

Edward walked up to the cop and asked the tall, Irishman a couple of pointed questions.

-What time is it, Officer?

The Police Officer looked at his wristwatch.

-Just going on 6 o'clock in the morning on this beautiful May day.

It was May!

-Officer? What about the year?

-I don't get you, young man. Why, it's 1947. What else would it be?

The Police Officer's Irish brogue was thick and downright jovial.

-Thank you so much.

Edward turned to Irene and embraced her.

-My God, we made it. Let's get to the Flatiron Building and see if the others are there.

The two people smiled all the way to 23rd St. and the Flatiron Building. When they reached the main entrance, they stopped smiling, thinking of the enormity of the task ahead of them. Edward leaned against the brick facade and took out a cigarette. He lit up. Irene stood just in front of him.

-Well, baby, where are the others?

-I'm sure that they made it. If we did, then they must have. They must be nearby. We must be patient.

A voice to the side of them answered.

-New boyfriend, Irene?

It was Roger Lee. His smile was cold and calculating.

-Well, cat got your tongue? Huh?

-Roger, you made it.

Irene was almost happy at seeing the gangster...almost.

-Apparently. But, what are you doing here? Did you smuggle yourself aboard?

-In a manner of speaking, yes.

-Why? Don't answer. I know why: to keep an eye on me.

-Don't flatter yourself, Roger. I thought that my scientific knowledge could help.

Roger Lee laughed out loud.

-And, I'm expected to believe that?

-I don't care what you believe.

Edward cut into this little argument.

-Hey, Lee, have you seen Lt. Donovan?

-No. I have not. I gather that you haven't either.

Edward flipped his cigarette into the street.

-He oughta' be along soon and, then, we can get organized.

-Edward?

-What is it, Irene?

-Just before we left, I realized that your father's plan is the only one that will save us.

-How's that?

-Yes, Irene, tell us mere mortals about your scientific revelation.

-I don't need your sarcasm, Roger. But this is what I realized. We...all of us...made a serious miscalculation. Earth was not the only planet shifted from its orbit. The orbits of the other eight planets were also affected, especially that of Mercury and Venus. Both of these planets are on an outward trajectory and even faster than that of the Earth because of their closer paths of revolution about the sun.

Edward picked it up.

-So even if the Earth's orbit is corrected, Mercury and Venus just might catch up with us and collide.

The P. I. pounded one fist into the other. Irene continued

-Yes. But it wouldn't even have to be a collision to wreak havoc. A near miss would be good enough to annihilate the Earth.

Roger took out a cigarette, but didn't light up. He did put it in his mouth, though.

-So, we're the last line of defense: the Earth's only hope. Mankind's depending on us to save its collective ass.

Irene looked at her former boss with disdain.

-Crudely put, yes, Roger. But- Oh!

-What is it?

Roger Lee spun around. It was Lt. Donovan coming up to the small group. He was grinning. He addressed Roger Lee.

-We're about to save someone's ass?

Edward lit another Lucky Strike.

-You bet...about three billion of 'em.

TWO

THE FOUR people sat at a corner table in a diner just off of 21st and Broadway. Edward was familiar with the place. It had good food at a pretty good price; nothing fancy, just your basics for the three essential meals of the day. They were sitting down to the diner's breakfast menu: pancakes, toast, bacon and coffee.

-Good coffee, Mr. Mendez. Do you come here often?

-Not as often as I'd like, Mr. Lee. Glad you like the coffee. Service isn't half bad either.

Lt. Donovan was finishing the last of his buttermilk pancakes.

-Didn't realize how hungry I was.

Irene was the only one not drinking coffee because she hated the stuff. She was having a soft drink, instead. She noted that her soft drink had just as much caffeine in it as did the gentle-men's coffee.

The waitress took away the plates and, then, came back to refill the coffee cups.

-Okay, I think it's safe enough to talk here. We have twenty-four hours...well, a little less now...before we're "pulled" back to our own time.

Lt. Donovan finished the P. I.'s thought.

-And, we have three people to bump off. That's a pretty tall order even for a trained assassin.

Roger Lee, with another unlit cigarette in his mouth, added this to the conversation.

-You must be more discreet, Lt. Donovan. We have three people to eliminate from the history books.

Irene spoke to Edward with a distinct hardness in her voice.

-Their names, what are they? We should put a name to our intended victims. One must know one's enemy.

Edward supplied the names.

-Heinrich Weiss. Karl Fassbinder. Miss Lisa Pabst.

-A woman? We have to kill a woman?

Roger Lee laughed at Irene's apparent dismay.

-Shocked, Irene? Maybe, we should leave that one for you, eh? Think you can pull it off?

Irene put down her glass.

-No. I'm not sure that I could do it. But, you could, Roger. I know that. She'd be only another victim for you.

-Easily.

Lt. Donovan leaned forward in his chair. He was anxious about several things, not the least of which was getting started.

-We have to locate these people first. And, that might take time that we don't have.

The Lieutenant addressed Edward.

-Mendez, this is right up your alley.

-It is. First order of business: eliminate the obvious.

-Meaning?

The P. I. put his hands in the air.

-We look in the local phone books. The A.T.&T. Building is right across from my office downtown. We can start there.

-Sounds like a plan. But, isn't that getting a little too close to your "present" self?

Edward had to agree, but...

-It's a chance we've gotta' take. Let's go.

The P. I. made to stand up and, then, remembered...

-We've gotta' use the subway, again. I can't use my car and neither can you, Donovan.

-I get what your mean. And, I can't set foot in the 86th. We're handicapped.

Roger Lee sat back and smiled.

-Gentlemen? And lady? Then, I think we had better get moving. And, just one more thing.

-Make it fast.

-Don't rush me, Lt. Donovan. When this is all done and we're back in 1950, I walk a free man. I know that it has already has been said, but it needs repeating After all, we will all be fellow cold-blooded murderers, no matter how you look at it.

Edward and Lt. Donovan exchanged glances, both men were now standing. Roger Lee continued.

-Do we agree to my fair and simple term?

-As you said, Mr. Lee, Mr. Manuel Mendez has already agreed to it. But, I'll agree to it now if that makes you happy. That is, if you get your target.

Roger Lee lit his cigarette.

-I have no scruples about killing an enemy. None.

He turned to face Irene.

-Want to come with me?

-No. I'm not falling for your charm. I know what your capable of, Roger. And, I don't want a knife in my back.

-I wouldn't do that, Irene. No. You misjudge me. I would slit your throat...give you a chance to defend yourself.

Edward broke into this discussion.

-That's enough of that. Irene comes with me. Got that, Lee?

-Whatever you say, shamus.

Lt. Donovan paid the check and the four people headed back into the subway.

The A.T.&T. Building was empty at this time of day. Lt. Donovan picked up a phone book and started paging through it. Edward, Irene and Roger did likewise.

-Karl Fassbinder lives right here in Manhattan. Shall I take him out?

-Hold up just a second, Lee. Here's Heinrich Weiss. He lives right here on Gold St. Mendez? What about Lisa Pabst?

Edward looked up from the thick phone book. He closed it with a thud.

-She's not listed in the Manhattan directory. I'll try the other boroughs. But, is she married? Pabst might be her maiden name.

Irene touched the P. I.'s arm

-I got the impression from your father that she wasn't married. Don't forget, she's a scientist and a Nazi. You try the Bronx, Edward, while I look in the Brooklyn directory.

Roger Lee was now sitting in one of the many phone booths leaving the accordion door open.

-Let's not forget Staten Island...as desolate as it is.

Before he could say anything more, Irene exclaimed.

-Here it is, Edward. Lt. Donovan. I found Miss Pabst. She's listed in the Brooklyn phone book.

Roger Lee, still sitting in his phone booth, laughed.

-How insulting, Irene. Leaving me out? Better not. Team work, remember?

Edward jotted down Miss Pabst's address in his notebook: 819 Wilson Ave., near his sister Dottie's old neighborhood. Karl Fassbinder lived in a boarding house on the upper west side right off of 72nd St. near Central Park

-Okay, Mr. Lee, mind joining us?

-Of course, Edward. My pleasure.

He got up and joined them at the phone book directory stand. Edward gave the instructions.

-Okay, Mr. Lee? You take Mr. Heinrich Weiss. Should be easy pickings. It's just a couple of blocks north of here. And, don't get caught.

Roger Lee smiled in mock appreciation.

-That's the first law of the jungle. You sound like a practiced assassin, shamus. I like that. I think you're a cold-blooded killer like me. I could use you in my syndicate. Why am I not surprised?

Edward ignored this remark and continued.

-Donovan? You take Fassbinder. He's just across town from your Precinct.

-I know the lay-out. I pounded a beat in that area a while back.

Irene addressed her question to the P. I..

-And, what about us, Edward?

-Miss Lisa Pabst, Irene. I've never killed a woman before.

-So why start now? It might be hard for you to do.

-It might.

Roger Lee put up both hands.

-The shamus is testing himself. Listen. This may look easy on paper, but killing is not easy. Yes. I know. We must begin at once. And, don't forget, these Nazis may have bodyguards assigned to them.

Lt. Donovan agreed

-Lee, here, is right about that. Problem is, we can't afford to be too careful.

Irene took Edward by the hand.

-Let us begin. We're wasting time here just talking. What more is there to say?

-Man, I wish I could use my office, but I'd probably run into myself.

-Irene, you're a scientist. What would happen if Edward Mendez, P. I. shook hands with Edward Mendez, P. I.?

-It's nothing to joke about, Roger. It could be cataclysmic. It might cause a time distortion that couldn't be corrected. But, honestly, I don't know. No one does.

Roger Lee smiled.

-I'll bet Manuel Mendez knows. I'd like to know where he gets his information.

Lt. Donovan posed a question.

-Hey, Mendez, why can't we use your office past working hours?

-That might work, but I think it's too risky. My old apartment back in Staten Island...now, that might work. I hardly ever went back there, but I did keep it up. We could use it as a rendezvous point.

-Give us the address, Edward.

The P. I. was getting just a little tired of that "sweet" tone of voice form Mr. Roger Lee. But, he wrote down his Staten Island address for each of them, just in case.

-Okay, it's a quarter of noon. We'd better get started. Chances are that our "targets" won't be at home.

Irene was perplexed.

-So much time has gone by. I hadn't noticed that it was almost noon.

Roger Lee spoke in answer to Edward's statement.
-But, our quarry *might* be home. One can never tell.
-Aren't we the optimist, Mr. Lee.
-The thrill of the hunt. It's the sportsman motto, no?
-I've heard of it. Never thought much of it, though.
Irene was growing restless.

-Please, let's go and get this over with.

They all agreed. Edward and Irene took the subway into Brooklyn. Lt. Donovan took the subway and headed uptown to the upper west side. And, Roger Lee started out toward Gold St., but maneuvered down to Wall St, instead. The gangster had plans of his own and these plans did not include the others. Yes. He would eliminate his target...eventually.

PRESENT TIME: 1950

A young teenage boy by the name of Romeo Duquesne was running through the streets of midtown Manhattan. He was afraid...afraid of being one of the many who would be killed by the oncoming asteroid. He had heard the news bulletin this morning. His reaction to it had been delayed by about three minutes...just about the time one has to make the most of a five cent phone call. His parents were at work. They worked the night shift. His mother was a short-order cook and his dad a night watchman in a downtown factory.

It was a beautiful, sunny day...a day that belied the horrific news that was still being broadcast hourly. Romeo ran down 57th St. between 6th and 5th Aves. There were other people who were also running through the streets like himself. Some were running in his direction and some in the opposite direction. Where should he hide? Was there any point in hiding at all? An asteroid the size of Australia? It was doomsday, all right. And, it was no asteroid. The young teenager knew that. He was up on his science fiction and science fact. It was a planetoid that was hurtling toward the Earth...a small planet that was gonna' smash the Earth to smithereens.

The subway...maybe, he should go down into the subway? No. To be buried alive or crushed to death? He ran toward Central Park. He ran like he had never run before. He wanted to cry but what the hell good would it do? Maybe, he should head to St. Patrick's Cathedral and start praying real hard? No. The place was sure to be jammed packed with people.

He stopped running to catch his breath. He looked up at the sky. The cobalt blue had changed to white and there were no clouds in the sky. Other people noticed this as well...some started screaming hysterically...some fell to the ground and wept...some covered their faces waiting for the inevitable.

Officer Morgan Andes was looking out of the window on the 22nd floor of the Flatiron Building. He didn't like what he saw. The mob down below was growing larger and more unruly. Tracy was standing next to him.

-I can hear them from all the way up here, Morgan. Should I be afraid?

-No. At least, not yet. They're probably gonna' move uptown to join the rioters there. But, just in case, stay away from the windows. Don't give them a target or a reason to enter the building.

Tracy moved away from the window. An angry Ginny Gray walked in and Tracy motioned for her to move back into the corridor. Tracy joined her there.

-Morgan doesn't want us near any of the windows. The mob down there is getting restless.

-I'll bet! I was just kicked off the damned roof by his nibs. Pompous ass!

-I wouldn't take that personally.

-I take *everything* personally. It's how I get ticked off and running.

Tracy leaned back against the wall.

-I wonder where they are now? What they're doing.

-They haven't done anything yet because we're still here and wondering about it!

Doomsday

THREE

LT. DONOVAN got off the train and emerged on to Broadway and 72nd St. He liked this part of town. It was composed mostly of middle-class, hard working people like himself. It was a bit run down, but it spoke of old New York. He fond himself standing in front of a newspaper kiosk that was displaying a variety of magazine and local newspapers. As a matter of fact, every New York newspaper was on display along with assorted candy bars, gum and cigarettes. The Lieutenant bought a pack of L&M cigarettes.. He needed a smoke. He needed to think and make sense of what he was committed to doing and what he, himself, was about. He took out a cigarette and lit up. Yep. No sense in putting it off. It was nothing to intellectualize about. He made his way to Karl Fassbinder's boarding house.

It wasn't far to walk. The boarding house was on Central Park West, almost abutting the park. The building was an old pre-WW I building: red brick that had blackened with the city soot and windows that sharply contrasted...clean and clear. The maintenance people were doing their job.

Lt. Donovan walked up the stoop and right into the building. The registration desk was to his right and a middle-aged man was tending it. He had salt-and-pepper hair and his cheeks and nose were rose red. He was thin, but had the beginnings of a pot belly.

-Yes, sir?

Lt. Donovan was direct in his question.

-I'm looking for a Mr. Karl Fassbinder.

-Not in at the moment.

-When is Mr. Fassbinder expected back?

-Couldn't say.

-What's his room number?

-Room 423. He's not in.

-You said that. Mind if I wait upstairs for Mr. Fassbinder in his room?

-Can't let you do that.

Lt. Donovan took out his I.D. The man behind the counter got nervous. He took a step back.

-He do something wrong?

-He *will* do something wrong if I don't stop him.

-Well, I guess you can go right on up then. Here's the key. Mind you, I don't know how long he's gonna' be.

-Do you know him at all?

-No.

-Not too friendly, huh?
-Not unfriendly.
-The quiet type?
-I guess you could say that.
-Does Mr. Fassbinder ever have any visitors?
-Every now and again.
-Who? And, how long has he been registered here?
-I'd say about going on three months. The "who" part, I can't answer. Mostly men, I think. But, a couple of times this Asian looking lady came asking for him.

-And, these visitors never gave any names? Come on, pal...put on that thinking cap.

-The lady's name was like a beer brand. You know...Rheingold...but it wasn't that.

-How about Pabst?

-That's it! A Miss Lisa Pabst it was.

-Good man. And, the gents?

-Germans and not very nice people. Bullies more like it.

-Names?

The clerk shook his head in the negative.

-Never gave any. Just ordered me, like, to call up to Mr. Fassbinder.

Lt. Donovan was satisfied with that answer. He knew when someone was telling the truth or deliberately leaving something out.

-Okay, I'm on my way up. And, don't tell Mr. Fassbinder that I'm waiting for him..I'd like to surprise the gent. And, thanks.

Lt. Donovan took the elevator up to the fourth floor, but he didn't head directly to Karl Fassbinder's room. He wanted to check out the fire exit that led on to the fire escape in the back of the building.

-Good.

The metal stairs looked solid enough and there was a drop ladder on the first level that led to a back alley and straight on to Central Park West.

Lt. Donovan closed the door. He checked the back stairs. The stairwells were not carpeted and the passage was dark.

-Hmm. Footsteps might be heard, but no one's too likely to get a good look at my mug.

He closed the door and headed to Room 423.

Lt. Donovan used the pass key to enter the small room. He was struck by the wallpaper.. It was filthy and peeling from the bottom. The throw rug was threadbare. The bed was unmade and there was an empty bottle of cheap whiskey on the side table.

-And, this is how a scientist lives?

There was a chair placed by the window, next to the radiator. The Lieutenant was about to sit down, but changed his mind. His first thought had been to shoot Karl Fassbinder as soon as he crossed the threshold, but he had to make sure that he killed the right man.

There was a closet opposite the bed. He opened the door and went through Karl Fassbinder's clothes...not that many: one gray suit, a trench coat and a pair of wing-tip shoes. There was a suitcase on the floor. Lt. Donovan picked it up and brought it over to the bed. He opened it and found mostly under clothes, a couple of ties and a shaving kit. He felt the lining of the suitcase.

-Here we go.

He felt papers in the lining. He ripped open the lining and out fell a folded manila envelope containing papers, diagrams and a map of Antarctica. The Lieutenant looked at the diagrams, but the documents were in German.

-I'll be damned.

Lt. Donovan gathered the papers and diagrams and put them back in the manila envelope, but not back in the cheap leather suitcase. However, he did close the suitcase and put it back in the closet. He sat down on the bed with the manila envelope resting on his lap. He took out a pen from his suit jacket and wrote an address on it: The 86th Precinct House, New York, N.Y. 20. Attention: Lt. William Donovan.

The Lieutenant smiled to himself.

-I wonder what time "ripples" *this* is gonna' cause?

He got up from the bed and left the hotel room. He closed the door just as the elevator arrived. A tall man stepped out and made his way to Room 423. The Lieutenant remained where he was standing. The tall man approached him.

-You have been in my room?

The tall man spoke with a heavy German accent. He saw the manila envelope that the Lieutenant was holding.

-What is it that you have there? Answer me, please.

Lt. Donovan reached under his jacket, placing his hand on his revolver. He asked the tall man one question.

-Are you Karl Fassbinder?

-I am. And, who are you? A filthy, stinking cop, no doubt.

Lt. Donovan didn't answer Karl Fassbinder. Instead, he took out his revolver and shot the man point blank between the eyes.

Karl Fassbinder was pushed back by the impact of the bullet at such close range. When his body stopped its backward momentum, it fell to the ground.

Lt. Donovan acted by sheer reflex. He was a survivor and trained police officer who had also served in the Army. He kicked open the hotel room door and dragged Karl Fassbinder by the legs into the room. He placed him face down on to the bed. He threw a blanket over him and left the room with the manila envelope under his arm.

PRESENT TIME: 1950

-For a moment, I almost forgot why we were here today, mother.

-*Yes*. I had that same feeling. I wonder if it could be a sign from the past...a sign that things are going as they should.

-What else could it be? .

-We'll have to wait and see. How I loathe waiting. I should have insisted that I go with them. Why didn't I?

Susan ignored her mother's rather academic question.

-Time travel...so intriguing a concept. Yes, mother, maybe you should have journeyed with Edward.

Now, it was Marlena's turn to ignore her daughter's statement.

-And frightening. It gives rise to new definitions of the term. Does "time" exist at all or is it a perception that continues to elude us? We may never know. Do past events exist or are they simply a trick of one's memory? Does the universe actually exist as we perceive it?

-Good questions, mother.

Officer Morgan Andes wasn't thinking philosophical thoughts. His thoughts and concerns were much more practical. The mob across the street in the park was becoming more and more vocal. People were voicing their concerns in an ugly and crude manner. The mob was becoming unruly. Would they target the Flatiron Building or just head on uptown to Times Square? No telling what frightened and irrational people might do.

Officer Andes had his gun at the ready. He was prepared to use it. But, for just a moment, he forgot why he was reaching for his weapon.

FOUR

EDWARD AND IRENE were riding the elevated train into Brooklyn. It had just crossed over the Williamsburg Bridge and was approaching Greenpoint, a heavily populated Hasidim Jewish neighborhood. Irene noticed that Edward's attention had been diverted. The P. I. looked uneasy and anxious.

-Edward, what is it? Who are you staring at. Is it that blonde girl sitting over there by the window.

Edward turned back to face Irene. The look on the P. I.'s face was an incredulous one.

-Yes. That's Lorraine Keyes sitting over there.

-You mean the girl who was murdered on Sullivan St...or, should I say, will be murdered?

-Yes.

Irene grabbed a hold of the shamus' jacket.

-Edward, don't even think about approaching her.

-I wasn't...not really.

-You were. Her fate has been decided so don't tamper with it. If you warned her, she wouldn't believe you anyway.

-Aren't we already tampering with fate?

-A single thread of fate...and that's dangerous enough.

Edward took out a cigarette, but didn't light up.

-And, you don't know anything about the girl, not really.

Edward's P. I. gut instinct kicked in.

-What do you make of her, Irene. Give me your take from a woman's perspective.

The train stopped at Marcy Ave., the first stop in Brooklyn...or the last stop...depending on which direction one was traveling in. A few passengers got off, but no one got on. The doors closed and the train moved on.

Irene studied the girl with the intensity of another woman.

-She's strange. Pretty but...she wears no adornments and very little make-up. Her black dress doesn't suit this time of day. And, her eyes...

Edward interrupted her.

-Irene, what time have you got? My watch has gotta' be off. It can't be this late.

Irene looked at her wristwatch which doubled as a bracelet.

-I have 1:45 P.M., Edward. But, how can that be? We left the Flatiron Building just after 11:45 A.M. It wasn't that long ago, was it?

The P. I. shook his head, grinning.

-Time, Irene. We're violating time and it's passing us by. Didn't count on this, did we?

-If that's true...and it must be...then we have far less time than we thought.

-I just hope that Donovan and Lee are noticing this, too.

-I'm sure that they are. They're not stupid.

Edward looked out the window of the moving train.

-We're coming up on Broadway and Myrtle...from there, it's only another two stops.

-Good. We must go directly to Lisa Pabst's address. We've not a moment to lose.

-Irene, baby, you just said a mouthful.

They got off at Knickerbocker Ave and headed one block up to Wilson Ave. and Lisa Pabst's address.

-This is the address.

-It looks very working class.

-It is, Irene.

A woman was sweeping the sidewalk in front of the three story apartment building. She walked over to Edward and Irene still holding her broom.

-May I help you folks?

Her smile was genuine. She was a petite woman in her mid-forties. She was wearing a cotton house dress and slippers.

Edward responded using his Latin charm.

-I hope so. We're looking for a Miss Lisa Pabst. Do you know her?

-Of course! She's our next door neighbor. My name is Francine Farmer, by the way. My two sons should be coming home from school any minute now. They go to the Catholic school nearby.

-Mrs. Farmer, is Miss Pabst at home now?

-Oh, no! She's a librarian. She'll be at work now.

-When is she expected home?

-You just missed her, Mr...

-Mendez. This is my good friend, Irene.

-Pleased to meet you both. You don't live around here, do you?

-No, we don't. Where is this library?

-Just walk straight down Wilson. It's across the street and to your right. Can't miss it.

-Thank you.

-Are you friends of Miss Pabst's?

Irene answered Mrs. Farmer.

-We know of Miss Pabst. We need to speak to her. It's urgent.

-She's not in any trouble, is she? She's very quiet...keeps to herself. Funny name for an Asian lady...Pabst.

Edward thought so, too.

-Is she married, Mrs. Farmer?

-I imagine she was. That would account for the last name, wouldn't it? But, she does live alone. Oh...here are my two boys! Please, excuse me.

-Of course. And, once again, thanks.

Edward and Irene passed the two boys and continued on toward the library.

-Edward?

-Yes?

-What's the plan? Do we kill her in public or wait until she leaves work? Can we afford to wait so long?

Edward looked real hard at his Asian companion. He pointed to the sky.

-Look. It's starting to cloud up.

-You're avoiding my question. I know it's not a pleasant one, but it's vital that we act quickly and...yes...mercilessly.

-I'd like to speak to Miss Pabst. I've got a few questions for her.

-What would you ask her.

-Why the hell is she here in Brooklyn of all places masquerading as a librarian? What's the point? If she's so vital to this Nazi death machine, why allow her to roam about like some ordinary "Joe?" Makes no sense. Wouldn't they have her under lock and key? I would.

-She might not be a willing participant to their plans. Maybe, they plan to kidnap her. Don't forget, the sun's disappearance is months away.

-So, they're giving her some false sense of security.

-It's possible, Edward.

-What do you think?

-I think that she's one of those "sleeper" agents. You know, the ones who lie in wait until they're called up. The ones who pass themselves off as everyday people who you'd never suspect of being anything but "normal."

Edward and Irene kept walking as the clouds overhead thickened and threatened rain.

-Look, Edward, that must be the library.

The library was a two story, brick building with two Roman columns on either side of the main entrance.

-Let's go in and introduce ourselves to Miss Lisa Pabst.

-Yes. Let's.

The main door was made of heavy oak with an over sized brass handle, but surprisingly it opened easily to even a light touch. Irene and Edward walked in and climbed six marble steps to the main floor. The checkout counter and the "adult" section were to their left and the "children's" section to their right, just opposite the librarian's station. The place was well lit with overhead lights and there were long, rectangular reading tables in both sections. Each station had three "walls" of bookshelves surrounding the tables. The index files were in front of the "adult"section.

Edward and Irene walked over to the main desk. The librarian behind the counter walked over. She was a slim woman of about fifty. She sported silver "permed" hair with a pair of reading glasses dangling from a chain around her neck. She wore a tailored navy blue suit. The expression on her face was not friendly.

-Yes?

The greeting registered below the freezing mark.

-We're looking for Lisa Pabst. We were told that she worked here.

-She does.

-May we speak to her, please?

-Miss Pabst is in the children's section being of assistance.

-Thanks.

The "children's" section was only a few feet from where they now stood. Edward glanced at his wristwatch.

-Irene, look...it past 4 P.M.

-I know. Time is getting away from us. Look over there, Edward, that must be her talking to that woman and child.

-Let's just stroll on over and browse the bookshelves.

As casually as they could, the two of them got as close to Lisa Pabst without invading her personal space. They could hear the librarian's every word.

-I'm sure that if he can get through Moby Dick, he'll have no problem with A Tale of Two Cities.

-I hope not. He's a good student, but poor in reading.

-I would take these two books for now. It's a good start. You don't want to overload the boy.

-Thank you.

-You're welcome. Just bring them over to the check-out desk. And, try to encourage this young man in his reading. Ask him questions about what he's just read. That will help motivate him.

The mother and son took the books over to the check-out counter leaving Lisa Pabst tidying the bookshelf. Miss Pabst was an an Asian lady no taller than five feet. She was a little broad in the "beam" but not over weight by any means. Her attire was a simple but well-cut black dress. She looked up at the two people standing near her.

-May I help you?

-Miss Lisa Pabst?

Miss Pabst straightened up, a little surprised that this stranger knew her.

-I am Lisa Pabst. Do I know you?

-No. I'm a private investigator, Edward Mendez. This is Miss Irene Wong who is a scientist.

-Oh.. I see. A private investigator and a scientist. What do you want with me?

Irene answered Miss Pabst's question.

-Are you not a scientist yourself, Miss Pabst?

Lisa Pabst was no longer friendly if not exactly hostile.

-Who are you? I don't know you. I don't have to answer your questions.

-Keep your voice down, Miss Pabst. Your colleague at the desk is looking over at us.

-Let her! She's a bitch.

Edward suppressed a smile.

-What's your field, Miss Pabst?

-I won't tell you. I don't know what you're talking about.

-I think you do.

-I won't stand here and listen to this.

Edward's tone was no longer friendly; it was civil but cold.

-Where are your Nazi friends, Miss Pabst...Dr. Pabst? And, why are you here in this dump of a library?

-And, your breath smells of stale cigarette smoke, Mr. Mendez. You smoke too much. Look at the fingers of your hand.

Lisa Pabst was backing away from Edward and Irene. And, Edward wasn't as reluctant as he had been about killing this woman. Still, he wanted to give her a chance.

-Let's step outside, Miss Pabst. We can talk more freely out there.

At that moment, Edward caught sight of a familiar face. It was Jamie. Irene noticed this and whispered to the P. I.

-I see her, too. She was the girl you took to the Flatiron Building. Don't even think of going over to her. We are still affixed to the grid line. This is why, I believe, that time is so rapidly "passing" us by. Keep your focus on nothing but our objective.

Lisa Pabst continued to speak as if she hadn't overheard any of the conversation between Edward and Irene.

-I'm getting off work soon. Let me finish up. I know...I know what you're getting at. I won't deny it, but how on earth did you find me?

The P. I. looked long and hard at Miss Pabst.

-It's a long story and real complicated. But, you have to help us save the world – like it or not.

-I don't understand. You talk in riddles.

But, Miss Pabst's reaction told both Edward and Irene otherwise. This woman knew the import of Edward's words.

The P. I. continued to smile, but his eyes held a deadly warning.

-You're going to leave with us, Miss Pabst. Make your excuses to your superior over at the desk. Is that she over there...the woman we spoke to?

-Yes. She won't be pleased.

-Too bad. Tell her that an emergency's come up and that you'll make up the time Do it now, Miss Pabst. You see...I'm holding a gun on you and one word of a double-cross and you're dead. Savvy?

The hard tone of Edward's voice surprised even the P. I. He meant what he said. Irene looked on with grim approval.

-Move. You're taking too long.

-All right. I'll do what you say.

Miss Pabst walked over to the librarian's desk. When she got there, she placed both hands palms down on to the desk. And, without preamble...

-I must leave, Miss March. Something has come up and I have no time to explain. I'll just get my handbag and go. Of course, I will make up the lost time.

-Will we see you tomorrow, Lisa?

-I'm sure you will. Thank you. I must go.

Edward could see the skepticism on Miss March's pale, stern face. She didn't believe Miss Pabst's story, but she had no cause to sound an alarm.

The three people left the library and headed for Miss Pabst's apartment on Wilson Ave. Edward placed Miss Pabst between himself and Irene. Little was said en route, but Edward was formulating quite a few questions for his "hostage." He needed not only answers, but explanations. If three people had to be killed, the P. I. needed to know the essentials. Why all three? Couldn't at least one be spared? Did the method of execution justify the end result? It seemed to...almost. He had to know more.

-Here we are.

Irene looked sideways at the woman.

-We know. We spoke to one of your neighbors about you. She couldn't tell us very much. It seems that you keep to yourself.

-She doesn't know anything...only the facade that I've built around myself.

Edward was not impressed with that answer. It proved to him that Lisa Pabst was an adept liar.

-Let's go on in. We'll attract attention standing out here like this.

Miss Pabst led the way up to her third floor apartment. She unlocked the door and switched on the overhead light. They were in the kitchen. There was a small square table with a wooden chair on each side. A gas stove and refrigerator were to the left and the bathroom to the right. Past the Kitchen was the living room and, then, the bedroom. It was a back room apartment. The only window was in the kitchen facing on to the back alley.

Edward took charge.

-Okay. Let's all sit down. Miss Pabst? Sit across from me, if you would.

She did. And, Irene sat to Edward's left. Miss Pabst placed her handbag on the floor next to her. The P. I. found that strange. Why didn't she put the handbag on the table?

-Miss Pabst, is that your real name?

-Of course not.

The woman's demeanor had changed entirely. Her expression was severe and it matched the tone of her voice.

-Then, what is it? And, don't play fancy with me.

-Marguerite Schultz. And, what do you want of me? I'm not afraid of you.

-Good. Miss Schultz, what's your association with the Nazi Party?

-None of your damned business.

-Why are you living here...and under the guise of a librarian.

-Why do you say that it is a "guise?"

-Because you said it just outside.

-Maybe, I did. What of it?

-Edward, why are we wasting our time with her? Let's do what we came here to do. She's a hardened Nazi, can't you see that?

-Listen to her, Mr. Mendez. But, kill me and you learn nothing. And, you wouldn't like that, would you?

-I'm not liking you, lady, not one bit. What's your field of expertise?

-Quantum physics. I see no harm in telling you that much.

Irene's interest was sparked.

-Quantum physics? How so?

-You wouldn't understand, my dear.

-I'm a scientist like yourself. Try me. I'll let you know what I understand.

-Indeed. I call it particle conversion: the displacing of one object into another dimension...a dimension that is as real as the one that we exist in now. The Laws of relativity are suspended...a vortex is created...a tunnel if you would...leading through space and time. One could travel from one end of the galaxy to the other...or into another dimensional space/time continuum.

-Can we reverse such a process.

-Yes. I have the mathematical theory to back it up...on paper, anyway.

Edward asked a pointed question.

-Have you shared this information with anyone?

-A few colleagues.

-Give me names, Miss Pabst.

Miss Pabst hesitated.

-No. That I will not give you.

Irene posed both a statement and a question.

-Werner Heisenberg? He'd be interested in your theory, surely.

-Perhaps.

-Miss Pabst, have you been approached by anyone to put your theory to practical use? Someone who may have the apparatus to execute it?

Silence. Edward continued...trying to bait the scientist.

-I think you have. Were you told to wait...until you were called up?

Silence.

-I can't hear you, Miss Pabst.

-How could you? I didn't answer you.

-I could turn you over to the authorities.

-On what charge? My papers are in order. That was a hollow threat, Mr. Mendez. You can do better than that.

Edward leaned forward in his chair.

-Miss Pabst? If putting your theory into practice meant endangering mankind, would you still do it?

-I despise hypothetical questions. They have no meaning.

Edward persisted.

-Would you?

-As a scientist I must take risks of life and death.

-When are they coming for you, Miss Pabst.

-Soon.

Edward sat back and almost smiled. Miss Pabst was furious with herself.

-You got that out of me. Swine!

She spat on the floor.

Edward just shook his head at this foul woman.

-Sorry, Miss Pabst, but I can't let that happen.

-Oh? And, what can you do about it, Mr. Mendez?

Edward hesitated, but Irene didn't.

-Edward, you know what has to be done. Look. Look at the time. It's almost 10 P.M.!

The P. I. took out his Waltham. But, as he did so, Miss Pabst reached down for her handbag. She flipped it open. Irene saw this and slapped Miss Pabst hard across the face.

Edward stood up, knocking over his chair. He pointed his gun at Miss Pabst's forehead. He fired point blank, blowing off the top part of her skull. Blood splayed on to Irene, but not Edward because the force of the impact blew Miss Pabst's brain matter and blood away from him. The victim slid off her chair and on to the linoleum floor.

-Irene? Go clean yourself off in the bathroom over there. I'll take care of our friend.

Irene went into the bathroom. She found a sponge and dabbed at her dress to remove the blood stains and brain bits. Edward dragged the body into the bedroom and pushed it under the bed. He, then, went back into the kitchen and noticed that the overhead light was fluorescent. Miss Pabst went in for modern fixtures.

He called out to Irene.

-You about done?

-Almost. Just give me a minute to fix my face.

Edward smiled in spite of himself. The kitchen floor was stained, but what of it? He had a feeling that Miss Pabst didn't have too many visitors.

Irene emerged from the bathroom wiping her face with a towel.

-Edward? Her handbag? Shouldn't we go through it?

-You'd make a good detective. She was reaching for something just before I blew her skull to smithereens.

The P. I. reached down and placed the bag on the table. He opened it. The first thing he saw was a small handgun. Not too good for distance, but lethal at close range. Edward took it out and offered it to Irene.

-Might come in handy. Irene? You know how to use a gun?

-Yes. I do. Roger taught me.

-Here you go. Put it in your handbag. Every girl should have one.

-You might be right about that, Edward.

Edward took out Miss Pabst's wallet. It was stuffed with twenty dollar bills.

-Must be at least $400 here. She carried a lot of change around with her.

-Edward, we must take it. Let the police think that this was a robbery.

Reluctantly, the P. I. pocketed the money.

-Not much else, Irene. Keys, lipstick...compact. Let's look around. See if she kept any notes.

-Do we have the time?

-No. But, we better do it anyway. She may have drawn up notes and diagrams that she hasn't yet given over to her cohorts.

Edward and Irene went through dresser drawers, pulling them out and checking the undersides. They checked under the mattress and the box spring and found nothing.

-This doesn't make any sense. I'm a scientist. I have notebooks and journals everywhere.

-Let's check out the bathroom.

-You do that, Edward. I'll check the kitchen cabinets.

Edward was the one who hit pay dirt. Just behind the medicine cabinet, he noticed a hook that separated it from the wall. He unhooked the cabinet and placed it in the bathtub. On the wall was sheets of notepaper that almost went flying to the floor. He grabbed a hold of them.

-Hey, Irene? You can quit looking. I think I found them.

Irene rushed in, took the notes from Edward and leafed through them.

-I'll need time to study them.

-I saw an over-sized envelope in the bedroom. Let's put them in there and high tail it back to the city.

Irene looked at her wristwatch.

-It's just going on midnight. Edward, this is quite unnerving.

-Time just flies by when you're having a good time.

Neither one of them laughed.

Once outside, they headed directly for the elevated train back to Manhattan. They were the only ones walking the streets and it was an eerie feeling. The air was still...so still that one couldn't detect the faintest breeze. Overhead, there was a three-quarter moon. It was "milky" white as vaporous clouds passed in front of it.

Edward and Irene reached the elevated train station. They climbed the stairs and deposited their tokens into the turnstile. There was an elderly token clerk on duty who looked as if he were in a trance; not once did he look at them.

They climbed another flight of stairs to the train platform and waited...not knowing that they both had the same thought. Edward was the first to give it substance. The two of them were standing near the edge of the platform.

-Hey, Irene?

-Yes. And, I know what you're going to say.

-How come no one heard the gunshot?

-They might have and were too afraid to do anything; that's a very common reaction.

-When we left the building, I didn't see any apartment light on, did you?

-I know. I noticed that, too. I really can't explain it. But, let's not question our luck. It's been pretty good so far.

Edward rubbed his chin. He needed a shave.

-Yeah. I noticed that. Maybe our being in a different time frame put things and events out of sync.

Irene smiled up at the handsome man.

-Edward, you sound like a scientist. You'd make a good one. Have you ever thought of it?

-Nope. Lousy in math. And, here comes our train. But, this time separation or whatever you call it has got me worried...big time.

-Why?

-Are we going to be able to step back into the "right" time?

-According to your father, it should be simple.

-My father's no scientist.

-But, he's the closest thing to a scientist. He's an occultist...an art even older than science.

-True enough. He'd know about the elements and so-called other dimensions that Miss Pabst was talking about.

Their train pulled in and they got on. The car was empty so they sat by one of the windows. Edward looked over at his beautiful companion.

-Hey, Irene? You puzzle me just a little bit.

-Oh? How so?

-You can be quiet and sweet one minute and, then, the next...cold and calculating. Mind you, I'm not criticizing...just observing a fellow assassin.

Irene laughed.

-Yes. You know that you and Mr. Roger Lee think alike, at least a little bit? He's often mentioned my multiple personalities and how he's tried to figure them out. I've told him not to bother. I can't even figure them out.

Edward nodded and accepted this explanation. What else could he do? He wasn't the girl's psychiatrist.

-And, Edward? I have a personal question for you. I couldn't help but notice that you have a new girlfriend. She's very pretty.

-Thanks.

-You have good taste in women. What happened to Yolanda, if you don't mind my asking? Did the relationship come to an end or was it ended?

-I got dumped. Does that answer your question?

-Most men wouldn't admit that. But...you're not like most men. I admire that. It sets you apart. Miss Estravades was foolish in leaving you. She'll live to regret that, I'm sure.

They rode on for a few more minutes in silence. Edward was deep in thought. Just maybe Yolanda was right in finding herself a new man. After their last phone call, it had taken him all of forty-five minutes to pick up and shack up with the first pretty girl he happened on. And...the next day, he had a new girlfriend. His recovery time was pretty damned fast...maybe a little too fast?

Irene broke into Edward's thoughts.

-Edward, I wonder how the others are doing.

-I trust Lt. Donovan even if he doesn't always trust me. I'm not so sure about Mr. Roger Lee.

-Yes. No one can be sure about him, except to know that he's cunning and ruthless.

Edward smiled ant took out a cigarette, even though he knew it wasn't permitted to smoke on the New York City transit system.

-We were kind of ruthless ourselves, baby.

-One must be, Edward, in order to survive in a ruthless world.

Irene glanced at her wristwatch. It read: 1:30 A.M. It was less than five hours until their time was up in 1947.

FIVE

ROGER LEE came out of the gymnasium sauna sweating profusely. He toweled his naked body dry and, then, wrapped the same towel about his waist. He headed for the shower area. He climbed the two steps leading up to it and was now walking barefoot on the white tiled floor. He took off the towel and hung it on one of the metal hooks affixed to the wall. He turned on the shower to ice cold. Yes. It's just the shock his body needed. Now, he could go about his assigned task...to murder a Mr. Heinrich Weiss.

For most of the day, which seemed to be going by far too quickly, he'd consulted with his stock broker. He was making heavy investments in certain companies whose stock he knew would go up. He'd borrowed heavily from the bank and had put up several of his nightclubs as collateral.

He turned off the shower head and reached for his towel. He exited the shower area and glanced at the clock on the wall.

-Fuck! It can't be 1:30 A.M. already. Something's gone haywire, but I don't have time to figure it out.

Roger Lee flung the towel into the laundry bin. Naked, he hurried over to his locker and got dressed. He finished dressing and slammed the locker door shut without bothering to lock it. He went upstairs and checked out of the gymnasium.

Outside, it was warm with a sultry breeze coming from the south. Roger Lee looked around. The Chinatown streets were busy as usual, but he noticed a glazed look in people's eyes.

-Too preoccupied with life.

But, this observation troubled him.

Roger Lee started walking south toward Gold St. It wasn't far. He hoped fervently that Mr. Weiss was at home enjoying his last moments on Earth. He felt no sympathy for the man.

-Nothing but a stinking Nazi. It'll be one less for the world to worry about. And, it'll mean survival for about three billion people. If I weren't one of those three billion, I wouldn't give a damn.

And, he wouldn't.

The walk to the business district was fast and pleasant. How quickly and abruptly environs changed in Manhattan. The business district contrasted sharply with that of Chinatown. It was as if Roger Lee were alone in the world. Not the most comforting feeling for this gangster.

Doomsday

He was now walking down Gold St and looking for Mr. Weiss' address. He found it: a new apartment building. He opened the front door and was met by a doorman.

-Heinrich Weiss.

-Is Mr. Weiss expecting you?

-No.

-I'll ring him up.

-You do that.

-And, your name, sir?

-Benson Kwan. But, he won't know me. Just tell him it's about Antarctica.

-About what?

-He'll understand. And, mind your own business.

Heinrich Weiss answered the doorman's call on the first ring.

-Who? I know no such person. What?

Heinrich Weiss had to collect his thoughts. He was not expecting visitors much less someone who knew...

-Send him up. Thank you.

The doorman put down the house phone and turned back to Roger Lee who was already finding his way to the elevator bank. The doorman yelled after him.

-Make a left at the wall.

Roger Lee ignored him. He found the elevator bank and pressed the "up" button. He didn't need the apt.

number because he'd spotted it looking over the doorman's shoulder. He rode the elevator up to the 4th floor. He got off and walked over to Apt. 4B.

Roger Lee rang the doorbell. It was answered by a man of medium height and build. He was dark complected with short, wavy hair. His trousers were a cream color and his shirt sleeves were rolled up. He also had a gun pointed at Roger Lee.

-Who are you? And, what do you want?

-Put that gun away and I might tell you.

-Get in here. That's it. Now, close the door with your foot. Good. Turn around.

Heinrich Weiss frisked Roger Lee. He took the gangster's gun from his belt.

-Now, face me.

Roger Lee was fuming...waiting for the first opportunity which would surely come.

-Stay there.

Heinrich Weiss had also taken Roger Lee's wallet and was now glancing nervously through it.

-You carry quite an amount of cash on your person, Mr. Lee. You a gangster?

Roger Lee smiled and shrugged his shoulders, but didn't answer.

-Now, don't move. I must call an associate of mine.

Heinrich Weiss fumbled with the phone on the end table. He finished dialing and picked up the receiver.

-Hello? This is Heinrich. I need your help. An intruder is in my apartment. No. I have things under control, but I don't like the look of him. Roger Lee. Name means nothing to me either. I don't know what he's up to. Of course, I will question him. Good. Hurry.

He put down the receiver...and Roger Lee, who'd been watching the man's eye movements, saw the instant that Mr. Weiss looked away. The Chinese gangster acted. Roger Lee gave a round house judo kick that caught Mr. Weiss square in the groin. The Nazi doubled up in pain, dropping his gun to the floor. Roger Lee scooped it up and landed a karate chop to the back of Heinrich Weiss' neck. He emptied Mr. Weiss' gun and now held his own gun on the Nazi.

-You in pain, Mr. Weiss? Don't bother to answer. I want you to crawl to the door on all fours. Think you can do that for me?

Heinrich Weiss managed to choke out an answer.

-I will not crawl for you or for anyone. Kill me. I am prepared to die.

-We're wasting time. And, your pious speech doesn't impress me. Who were you talking to on the phone just now?

-Go to hell.

-You're going there first. Get up.

-No.

Roger Lee kicked Heinrich Weiss in the ribs. The Nazi was on his back and writhing in pain. Roger Lee ripped the phone cord out of its socket. He tied Weiss' hands behind his back, forcing him up to a standing position.

-Let's go, pal. We're taking a short trip to the roof. Move.

Roger Lee pushed his victim forward and out of the apartment, taking the apartment keys with him. He locked the door and pushed Mr. Weiss to the elevator. He pressed the "up" button, careful to keep his victim out of sight in case the elevator doors opened and there was a passenger inside.

The elevator door opened and there were passengers inside.

-Sorry. Meant to ring the "down" button.

Damn it!

-Hey, Weiss? You and I are taking the stairs. You look like you could use the exercise.

Roger Lee propelled his hapless victim to the stairwell. It was a six story climb to the 10th floor and then a ladder up to the roof. Heinrich Weiss was winded and tears were streaming down his face when he collapsed on to the tarmac.

Roger Lee walked over to the edge of the roof and looked down. He was satisfied that the fall would be fatal. He walked back over to Mr. Weiss.

-Get up.

No movement.

-Get up, I said.

No movement.

Roger Lee kicked Mr. Weiss so hard that the man fell over on his side.

-I'll just have to roll you over.

Roger Lee kept kicking and shoving his victim. He didn't stop until he reached the edge of the roof.

-Over you go. Don't be too afraid. I've heard that falling from a high place is like being motionless in midair.

Regina King was driving her new, white convertible. She'd had it for a couple of days, but this was the first time she was showing it off in this part of town. She wanted to impress people...the right people. She slowed down as she approached the traffic light.

Miss King heard the updraft of air as Heinrich Weiss came hurtling down ten stories. He hit the pavement three feet from her stopped car. The impact was horrific...blood and brain matter were splayed across the pavement and on the passenger side of Miss King's convertible. Blood splashed on to Miss King who for a split second couldn't comprehend what was happening. In the next second she knew what had just happened...and screamed.

Roger Lee was laughing until he looked across at the horizon.

-What the hell is this? The sky is starting to get brighter. It must be close to sunrise. But, that can't be.

He looked at his wristwatch. It read 5:00 A.M.

-Something is very wrong here.

He made for the exit.

PRESENT TIME: 1950

Marlena Lake and Susan Broder found themselves alone on the 22nd floor of the Flatiron Building. They knew that they had to be there but the exact reason eluded the two women.

-Are we the only ones in the building?

-Maintenance must be here...somewhere. And, there must be a guard on duty.

-I keep thinking that Edward will be coming down that flight of stairs at any moment, mother.

-What makes you say that? Not that I doubt your feelings.

-I'm at a loss to explain it. I really can't.

-Yes. I know what you mean, in a manner of speaking.

Romeo Duquesne finished getting dressed. It wasn't even 6 A.M., but he was ready to go out. And, yet, he had the feeling that he'd been outside already. Why did he keep thinking of Central Park and even midtown? He couldn't figure it.

Doomsday

His parents had arrived home from work and were preparing to eat their main meal of the day. He usually joined them to have his breakfast, but would they have bad news for him today? Had they heard something over the radio...some emergency news bulletin? If so, he didn't want to know about it.

He went downstairs to the kitchen. His Mom and Dad were there and they seemed happy enough.

-Good morning, Romeo. How about some pancakes?

The teenager smiled at his Dad...relieved.

-Love some. And, you wouldn't believe the dream I just had. It was so real that it had to be more than just a dream. The world was coming to an end and I was running scared...real scared. And, at the last second, it didn't happen. I was back in my bed.

Romeo's father, Quentin Duquesne, looked real hard at his son.

-Funny you should talk about dreams. Me and your Mom had similar dreams last night...and they weren't pretty.

-Like what?

-We couldn't get home from work because the subway had been shut down.

-Why was it shut down?

-Because it was being used as a shelter for civilians. It was pretty frightening...and the feeling of hopelessness was God-awful. It was like we were all waiting to get wiped out.

Romeo felt a chill go down his spine.

-Like what was gonna' happen, Dad?

-The end of the world was coming.

SIX

THE SUN was about to rise on the horizon and Lt. William Donovan was looking out on the city atop the roof of the Flatiron Building. The 86th Precinct should be getting the envelope that he mailed some time early tomorrow morning. "Lt. Donovan" should be receiving it...placed on his desk by whom? Sgt. Rayno who was still alive? Alexandra Raymond who was just starting out at the Precinct? Didn't matter. It would be handed over to the Dept. of Defense.

It was getting hot on the roof. Where were his fellow assassins? Had they been successful or possibly even arrested? There was always that danger. The Lieutenant was standing in the spot from where his time travel journey had begun. How long could he stay there without being noticed? Maintenance men could come up at any time and ask some pretty awkward questions. He looked at his wristwatch. It was nearly 6:00 A.M. Man, time was flying by, but what did that mean? He shook his head and wiped his brow with a handkerchief. Should he have gone to Mendez's place in Staten Island? Was there enough time for that? Probably not. In real time the trip out there would take an hour and a half...and an equal amount of time to get back. Three hours in "real" time. But what about the time that the four of them had intruded upon? Twelve hours...twenty-four hours or more? No. He couldn't take that kind of a gamble.

Lt. Donovan still couldn't believe what he had done: killed a man in cold-blood. And, it had been so damned easy. And, there was no guilt. None.

The rooftop door opened and Edward and Irene emerged. They walked over to the Lieutenant.

-Glad to see you, Lieutenant. Job done?

-Yes. And, you and Miss Wong?

-Yes.

Lt. Donovan nodded approval.

-Did you find any papers on Miss Pabst?

-Plenty. Irene has them in that envelope. When we get back, she'll go over them before handing them over to the Dept. of Defense.

Lt. Donovan wasn't sure if he liked that idea. After all, Miss Irene Wong was an illegal immigrant and could be deported at any time. But for now, he kept quiet about it.

-I mailed Fassbinder's papers to the 86th.

Edward smiled at the irony of that.

-To yourself?

Irene also smiled approvingly at the Lieutenant.

-That was very clever of you, Lt. Donovan. We must follow up on your course of action when we get back. It should prove interesting.

-It seemed like the right thing to do at the time.

Irene walked away from the two men, but not too far.

Edward asked the obvious question.

-Where's Mr. Roger Lee?

-Probably up to no good.

-Just so long as he's done his part.

-It wouldn't be hard for that hood. It sure wasn't too hard for me. It was almost too easy.

Edward grinned at the truth of that statement.

-I know what you mean.

Irene came back to the two men and pointed to the sky.

-Look at the sun. It's about to rise in the sky. Look at your wristwatch.

-What's the point?

-Miss Wong what are you trying to tell us?

She looked hard at the Lieutenant.

-Time is out of balance...or should I say, that we are caught outside its stream of motion. We must attempt to get back now. The twenty-four hours is almost up.

She looked toward the rooftop door with concern clouding her face.

-Where is Roger? He's holding us up. What can be keeping him?

The rooftop door swung open.

-Am I the last to arrive? I always did enjoy making an entrance.

Roger Lee walked over to the group. He showed no signs of anxiety.

-Irene? You looked worried. Have I caused you concern? Have I missed anything? You must fill me in. Please.

Edward spoke to him and didn't mince words.

-Don't be so damned flippant, Lee. We have to try and get back to 1950 before it's too late. Were you-

Roger Lee cut the P. I. off.

-Successful? Of course.

-Did you search for any papers?

-I ransacked the poor bastard's apartment.

He reached into his jacket pocket and took out a wad of note papers.

-Here. I looked through it. Means nothing to me. Maybe, Irene, here, can translate the math. Or maybe I can sell it on the black market? Could fetch a pretty good price.

Lt. Donovan extended his hand.

-Just hand it over, Mr. Lee. You'll be walking away a free man and that's payment plenty.

-Of course.

Doomsday

Roger Lee handed over the notes to the Lieutenant who put them in his jacket pocket. And, he asked a pretty vital question.

-Now, what? Just how do we get back to 1950? Not so far, really, when you think about it. Three years out of countless billions. Should be easy, no?

Edward answered him.

-If you know how, anything's easy.

-Then, tell us how, shamus. Or don't you know?

-Everyone go to your corner of the roof and look directly ahead.

Lt. Donovan and Roger Lee walked over to their respective "points."

-Irene? Stand right behind me. That's where you were, wasn't it?

-Yes.

-Okay.

Edward shouted to the other two men.

-Stand still and look directly ahead...but seeing absolutely nothing but eternity.

Lt. Donovan, Roger Lee and Irene tried to do as Edward instructed, but the rising sun caught their attention.

Edward saw this and shouted as loud and hard as he could.

-Don't lose your focus. Don't be distracted by anything.

The sun rose just above the horizon...and time sped by. The sun arched across the blue sky and set just as the moon rose in the night sky. It moved gracefully across the black velvety night...quickly...too quickly.

No one spoke as dawn beckoned...but only for a moment. The sun rose once more in the sky to disappear once again in the west.

And, then...the grid appeared. Each man and woman on that roof "walked" on the line that had no beginning and no end. Darkness and light lie ahead as a feeling of weightlessness overtook the four people.

How much time would pass before their time journey ended? Or would it never end? Each one walked on the grid that hold the universe together until they saw the rooftop from where their journey had started.

Part V
The Deserted City

-EDWARD, WHERE is everybody?

That was a question that the P. I. couldn't answer. He, together with Irene, Lt. Donovan and Roger Lee, were in their respective places on the Flatiron Building's rooftop. Lt. Donovan and Roger came forward as Irene continued to ask questions.

-Why is it so quiet? You can almost hear the silence in the very air. A city this size is never silent, not even in the dead of night. I know this to be true. It's pretty self evident.

Edward could only nod in agreement with Irene's questions and observations.

Roger Lee asked a question of his own, but to no one in particular.

-The sun is still overhead and I feel warm. Were we successful? I think we were...there's no damned chill in the air

Edward spoke his thoughts out loud.

-Or were we the sacrificial lambs placed atop the altar?

Roger Lee grew angry. He was afraid of the unknown. He was an ordered man who didn't like question marks thrown at him.

-Why the hell do you say that? You mean that we were pawns of your rotten father? A man we should never have trusted? Is that what you're saying, Mr. Private Investigator?

-Yes.

-How easily you say that, shamus. You don't mind being duped, huh? I mind it a great deal. Your father just better have my money to hand over when we get back. I don't do things for free.

Edward tried to reason with the gangster.

-Just calm down, Mr. Lee. Right now we don't know anything for certain.

Irene was looking out on the panoramic view of the city. The streets were empty. No pedestrians were moving about on the sidewalks below. Cars were parked, newspaper stands stood ready for business...but nothing moved...not so much as a bird in the sky.

Lt. Donovan made a suggestion.

-Let's head on downstairs. We can't do much of anything just standing around up here.

The others agreed with the Lieutenant. They walked toward the door and, then, descended the stairwell to the 22nd floor. Edward was the first one down.

-Anyone here?

No answer.

-Is anyone about?

No answer.

Irene touched the P. I.'s shoulder.

-Don't waste your breath. A miscalculation has been made...that must be it We were not in synchronization with the time pattern of 1947, but we were able to function within it, all the same. But, now-

-Keep talking, baby, we need answers.

-But, now, we seem to be lost within a fragment of a second...stuck between the ticking of a clock.

-Believe it or not, baby, I think I follow you. But, just how do we get unstuck?

-Edward, do you remember when we were in that town in Long Island?

-Smithtown? What about it?

-When you tried to reach the 86th Precinct and, then, Connie Fulton?

-I couldn't get through. What about it?

-Your sister, Dottie, was telling me about it and it struck me as very odd.

-It was *damned* odd, now that you mention it. But, why bring it up now?

-It's my belief...theory, really...that the anti-matter element put that town, for a brief time, in a different time-space continuum.

-Meaning, Irene?

That was Roger Lee asking that question and demanding an answer.

-That that particular area had been removed form the Earth and placed somewhere in an anti-matter world...possibly an anti-matter Earth.

-But the effect didn't last.

-Fortunately, no. It corrected itself because the anti-matter was limited to the one person carrying it.

-Angel Correa.

-Yes. And, he was destroyed. But, there might be some anti-matter material remaining. Perhaps, fragments of whatever made him that way.

-And, a fragment of anti-matter might've interfered with our time travel escapade?

-Yes. It disrupted our journey back and now it's trapped up in a prison of time. It's the only explanation that I can come up with.

Roger Lee shook his head in frustration.

-So, now what the hell do we do? We find this fragment or fragments? Smithtown is a wide open area. I should know. We could search for days and not find anything...assuming that your theory is correct.

Lt. Donovan fired off a few questions of his own.

-What happens when and if we do find this anti-matter fragment? What the hell do we do with the damned thing?

-We throw it into the chasm where Angel Correa was killed...into the abyss that's now a part of the sand pit.

Edward started walking toward the elevator.

-We'll need a car. We can use mine. It's parked right outside.

Roger Lee held back.

-Just hold up for a second. How do we know this is going to work? Shouldn't we take the fragment here to the Flatiron Building?

Irene put up her hand in protest.

-No! I'm sure that would disrupt the time element even further. We must toss it into the pit that Correa's death created and that should shield its effects and bring us back to our own time.

Roger Lee grinned in doubt.

-You hope. It sounds pretty far fetched to me.

-What else can we do? Please, Roger, give me an alternative.

-You've got me there, Irene. Okay. So, let's all pile into the shamus' car.

The four people entered the elevator. Edward brought it down to the lobby. They left the building and walked across the street to the P. I.'s DeSoto.

Edward started up the DeSoto and pulled out of the parking space. Irene was sitting up front with the P. I. and Lt. Donovan and Roger Lee were sitting in the back seat. There was no traffic except for the cars that were stopped in the middle of the roadway with no one inside them. Irene noticed this and found it quite disturbing.

-It doesn't make sense. We should be seeing people frozen in time perhaps...but-

-But, what?

That was Roger Lee.

-Tell us, Irene. But, what?

Edward offered an answer while maneuvering around a truck.

-Inanimate objects are visible, but not living, sentient things like human beings.

Irene agreed with the P. I., but his explanation caused her even more anxiety.

-I don't like it, Edward. It's as if the whole human race has been wiped out. Why inanimate objects and not living beings?

No one answered him, but Roger Lee persisted.

-But, where are the bodies? Dead bodies would no longer be animate, no?

Lt. Donovan joined in the conversation.

-Disintegrated? Vaporized? But, then, nothing would be left standing. I think it's what Miss Wong said before: we're out of sync. with time.

-Yes, Lieutenant, out of synchronization with the flow of time.

Edward was busy maneuvering around immobile cars to worry too much about theory and opinion.

-It's gonna' be tough getting out of the city. I think we might have more luck if I tried driving down West St., there's usually less traffic there.

He veered over toward West St. The "stopped" cars were fewer in number. Roger Lee approved.

-Good. We're making better progress.

Roger Lee caught himself staring at the back of Irene's head. He smiled.

-Irene, do you know you have gray hairs, my dear? Not as young as you make out, eh?

Irene turned around and glared at the gangster.,

-Just shut your mouth! And, take a good look at yourself. You're graying around the temples.

Roger Lee leaned forward to look at himself in the rear view mirror. He saw two things that alarmed him quite a bit. He was graying at the temples, but even more alarming...nothing was being reflected in the car's rear view mirror...no cars, no buildings...it was like looking into a blank mirror. He forgot his annoyance with Irene and pointed out this phenomenon to the others.

-Everyone, look in the mirror. Look!

Lt. Donovan and Irene both looked. Edward slowed down and also had a good look. They were all speechless. Irene was on the verge of tears. What had their time journey done to the world and to them?

Edward sped up, again...tight lipped and tight fisted. Lt. Donovan took out a cigarette, put it in his mouth, but didn't light up. He felt like spitting it right out.

Silence. No one spoke. For the moment, they simply stared straight ahead.

Lt. Donovan was thinking about one person: Alexandra Raymond. He missed this woman. He missed her composure and beauty and...yes...courage. Why hadn't he been more forthright with his feelings about her? If he got back alive, he'd have to correct that. He'd *want* to correct it.

Miss Irene Wong wanted recognition for her scientific genius. She wanted credit for theories and hard work. Too often, Professor Lange had taken public credit for much of the original work that she had done. She must correct that. And, she also needed remuneration...she was virtually broke. While working for Roger Lee and his various nightclubs, she had picked up the rather bad habit of gambling. Her intellect told her that it was a con man's game, but the urge to gamble had persisted. She owed money to some very dangerous loan "sharks."

Roger Lee had only one thing on his mind: getting the hell back to 1950 in one piece and check on his investments. He looked forward to it. As a matter of fact, he was so elated by his mastermind plan that he almost forgot about getting even with Irene. Almost.

Edward Mendez was focused on the job at hand. All other thoughts and daydreams were put on hold because nothing else mattered but getting back to 1950. If they got "stuck" where they were...well...it would mean dying of old age or maybe even something worse. Maybe, they'd be caught in some kind of back and forth time loop. He'd read about such things in those science fiction magazines that Morgan Andes had lent him. You keep repeating the same thing over and over again with no hope of ever getting out of it.

The P. I. shook that thought out of his head. Why borrow trouble? They had enough to worry about. He kept his eye on the road.

The DeSoto was now crossing over the Brooklyn Bridge. It took Edward a few minutes to maneuver around the "abandoned" vehicles, but it was easier than he thought it would be. And, the silence finally got to the him.

-So, how come the mirror's not reflecting anything except our faces? And, for that matter, why is my car even able to move? Irene, baby, you're the scientist here, how about some answers?

-A mirror is a reflection of matter placed before it. Anti-matter would not be reflected or...it would be reflected as actually perceived.

-You lost me.

-When one looks in a mirror, the actual image is reversed. Anti-matter would not be reversed.

Lt. Donovan shook his head and spoke up.

-And, what about a blank? What the hell does that mean, Miss Wong? This rear view mirror is reflecting *nothing*.

Roger Lee volunteered a series of questions that he hoped no one could answer.

-Then, we don't exist? Are we dead? Is this what comes after life? What about it, Irene?

-You're joking, Roger, but you might not be too far from the truth. We're caught between matter and anti-matter. We're on the "line"...that "thread...that Manuel Mendez spoke of. And, somehow we're stuck.

-How about my DeSoto, Irene?

-Perhaps, our presence within it draws it to that grid line. Edward, please I can only theorize.

Lt. Donovan spoke up. He was getting annoyed at all the talk going on.

-Let's just get over to Smithtown, pronto. We've got a lot of ground to cover when we get there.

Roger Lee persisted in one argument.

-Why is our hair turning gray? Are we aging? Why should we when we're supposed to be stuck in time. Irene? You have all the answers.

-You know, I'm sick of you, Roger. What do you want me to tell you? You want me to soothe your sensitive nerves?

Roger Lee didn't answer, but he did notice more gray hairs appearing on Irene and Edward. He turned to look at Lt. Donovan who was now almost completely gray. The Lieutenant caught Roger Lee staring at him.

-I know. I caught a look at myself in the mirror. We're aging and I'd say we're aging pretty rapidly. But, I don't feel weak...at least, not yet, anyway. I still feel-

-Virile?

-Yes, Mr. Lee. Like I can still get it up.

-That's a relief, no? But, how much time do we have?

The Lieutenant shrugged.

-Ya' got me. But, how the hell are we gonna' find this anti-matter piece?

Edward heard that last statement and answered Lt. Donovan.

-If I'm not mistaken, Detective Kinsella recovered it and it should be at his Precinct. I think... I know I overheard something like that when I was trying to get an outside line. I should have paid more attention. I just hope I heard right.

Roger made the sign of the cross.

-I'm not a religious man, but let's pray that it's there.

-Amen to that.

Edward drove past the blown-up model home and headed straight to Detective Kinsella's Precinct. The parking lot was empty and Edward thought that was unusual, but didn't say anything to his fellow passengers. They had enough to worry about. He parked in front of the main entrance and everyone got out.

-Okay. Lieutenant? You and Mr. Lee stay with the car. Irene and I will head inside. Let's make this fast because, like it or not, we're aging.

-Meaning?

-Meaning, Mr. Lee, we haven't got much time. Savvy? Unless you don't mind turning into dust. Irene, let's go.

Edward and Irene walked into the station house. It was empty. The silence in the room was like a pressure that one could actually feel...it was almost deafening.

-Edward, where would they put it? You must know.

-In the evidence room which should be straight ahead. They're a small unit so they don't have too many divisions.

Irene touched Edward's hair.

-Edward, you're completely gray.

-I hope it looks good on me.

Irene smiled up at the P. I.

-It looks very distinguished...even the age lines. You have a handsome future ahead of you.

-I hope I've *got* a future. Here we go.

Edward had to kick open the locked door to the evidence room. What they were looking for was resting on a wooden rectangular table. It was the box that had contained Angel Correa's wings. The exterior of the box was a muted color...sort of white mixed with a touch of silver.

Irene touched it.

-It's all right, Edward. It's safe enough. The container is not anti-matter. We must take it to the sand pit at once.

-What's inside of it? I want to check that out.

The P. I. lifted the cover, but not before Irene blurted out a warning.

-Be careful. Don't touch anything inside.

Inside the box was a metal frame that had the shape of wings. Edward grinned at the thing.

-So, this is where the Angel got his wings from.

-Edward...please close it.

He closed the lid and glanced at his hands.

-My God!

Irene stretched her hands toward Edward.

-Mine, too. They're old and wrinkled. Even my voice sounds different...a harsher tone.

-Let's head on out and hope to God this works.

They rejoined Lt. Donovan and Roger Lee who were waiting for them.

-You found it? How wonderful that something has gone right.

-Don't count your chickens yet, pal.

-One must always have hope, Lieutenant, no matter how tenuous.

They piled into the DeSoto and headed to the area of the sand pit. When they reached the edge of the woods, they had to get out and walk through the forest path...the path that Edward and Irene had fled for their lives from the Angel. The burnt out areas from the Angel's anti-matter were still visible.

-Isn't it dangerous to walk this path? Isn't it filled with dangerous anti-matter?

-No, Roger. You forget, that we are separated by a paroxysm of time.

-You can explain that one to me later.

-Of course.

Edward, who was carrying the container, pointed up ahead to a clearing.

-We're almost there...just a couple of more yards. And, I don't know about the rest of you, but I'm getting dog tired.

Irene agreed.

-I know what you mean. I feel quite winded, too, as if the energy were being drained from me little by little.

This brought a smile to Roger Lee's face.

-Irene, your hair is entirely snow white. It's really quite becoming.

-I don't need your sarcasm. Not now. Too much is at stake.

-I wasn't being sarcastic.

Doomsday

The four people emerged from the path and found themselves standing a few feet from the sand pit's edge. Edward spoke up.

-We need to get closer to the edge. We can't afford a near miss.

They walked the few feet to the edge. What they saw was a black abyss that reached to the Earth's core. Lt. Donovan wiped the sweat from his face with a handkerchief.

-Mendez, I'll take one end and you take the other.

-Okay. Man, am I winded!

-Let's go. On the count of three: one...two...three!

The two men flung the rectangular box into the center of the black abyss...and waited.

Edward was the first to react.

-My vision...it's clearing. I hadn't realized it was clouded over until now.

Irene explained.

-Cataract, Edward, brought on by age. One doesn't look forward to them.

She looked down at her hands.

-They're not as aged as they were a few minutes ago. And, my voice...

Edward steadied himself, almost falling into the sand pit.

-I feel off balance.

The others agreed as the world about them seemed to turn upside-down.

-Hey, Mendez, what the hell's going on?

Irene answered the Lieutenant, shouting to make herself heard.

-The grid line is shifting...the graph that the universe is balanced upon.

-Where does that leave us?

Before Irene could answer Lt. Donovan, everything went black.

.

Epilogue

EDWARD OPENED his eyes and found himself standing on the rooftop of the Flatiron Building staring straight at Manuel Mendez who had just slammed the door in Ginny Gray's face.

-You were gone for only an instant. You flickered from sight and came back.

-Where's Irene?

-I'm right behind you, Edward.

The P. I. turned about and saw the young and lovely Irene Wong standing right behind him. She pointed toward the other corner of the roof.

-Look. There's Lt. Donovan and Roger. And, Roger is where he should be.

The P. I. walked toward his father followed by the others. For a moment, no one said anything. Edward had to break that silence.

-Were we successful?

-Yes. Feel the warmth in the air and look across at the park...no mob is gathering. No emergency radio broadcasts have been made. At least, none that I am aware of. You've done it! You've breached time and changed the course of history. This is an epoch moment in the history of mankind.

Irene addressed Mr. Mendez and quite urgently.

-What other consequences are there? I must know. Have we upset history so drastically?

Manuel Mendez smiled at the Asian beauty.

-That will have to unfold with time, my dear Miss Wong. Certain consequential events relevant to the sun's disappearance will remain in most people's subconscious.

-Will anyone remember it all?

-Your attuned people will.

-Like whom?

-Marlena Lake and Susan, perhaps, even Ginny Gray.

-Are they waiting for us downstairs?

-No. The sun's disappearance was avoided so there was no reason for them to be here.

-I've gotta' see this for myself.

Edward opened the rooftop door and practically ran down the flight of stairs. Only Marlena and Susan were there. The P. I. was astonished to see even them.

-Marlena? Susan? Do you know why you're here?

-On a somewhat intuitive impulse. You went...somewhere, dear boy, and it had to do with the sun. Am I correct?

Edward took out a much needed cigarette.

-Bull's eye, Marlena.

-Details, dear boy. You know how I feel about details.

-It's a long and pretty complicated story, but it's sure one that you're gonna' love to hear..

Edward lit up and took a deep drag on his Lucky Strike. Susan smiled at him while waving the smoke away from her face.

-It sounds intriguing, Edward. Why don't we all go back to the townhouse for a somewhat early drink or even an early breakfast?

Footsteps were heard on the stairwell. Susan looked past Edward and saw Lt. Donovan coming down.

-Lt. Donovan, are you here, as well?.

-Miss Broder, you and your mother knew to be here, huh?

-Mother did. I just drove her here on her "wild" hunch.

Irene Wong followed the Lieutenant and then came Roger Lee and Manuel Mendez. Susan couldn't help but exclaim.

-But, what's going on?

She'd never seen such an improbable group of people.

Roger Lee spoke up, but to no one in particular.

-I must leave. I am excused, no?

Lt. Donovan responded and not kindly.

-Get the hell out of here, Lee. I've got both eyes on you. Just behave yourself in public. Now, beat it!

-Of course. I'll be careful not to cross your line of vision, Lieutenant. And, now, I'll take my leave. Mr. Mendez? You and I have unfinished business. Will I be seeing you later?

-Yes.

Roger Lee pushed past the others and stepped into the waiting elevator.

-Good riddance, pal.

Edward grinned at Lt. Donovan.

-He's up to something.

The P. I. turned to his father.

-Isn't he? I couldn't help noticing a little coziness between you and that thug. By the way, how did you contact Mr. Lee?

-It wasn't through the phone directory. I can tell you that much.

-Tell me more. How did you manage it?

Lt. Donovan joined in. He wasn't at all pleased about Roger Lee going free.

-Mr. Mendez? How *did* you manage it? I'd like to know.

-Am I under interrogation here?

-Not officially.

-Good. Then, I have no answers for either you, Lieutenant, or my son. Please excuse ,me, I'll be in my office down the hall making notes on our success. Edward? Lt. Donovan? Miss Wong? When it's convenient, I'd like detailed accounts of everything that transpired...everything you saw and heard and felt. Do you realize that time travel is now in our grasp? The very concept is staggering. I suggest that you all check the back pages of the various newspaper articles dating from the day after your sojourn into the past.

Edward responded to his father's suggestion.

-That's exactly what I plan on doing.

Susan spoke to Edward.

-Edward, please let me know if I can help. I'm pretty good at research.

-Yes. My daughter excels at research as do I.

Edward smiled at the two women.

-You're on.

The P. I. turned to Irene.

-Irene? Care to join us?

-Of course. But, I'm not sure where I'll be living. My lease is up and-

Marlena interrupted the Asian scientist.

-You will stay at my townhouse as my guest. It's been decided. And, I'll see to it that you're safe from the clutches of Mr. Roger Lee.

-He is dangerous, Miss Lake.

-You may call me Marlena.

Lt. Donovan made ready to leave. He was anxious to get back to the 86th and check on that packet of notes that he'd sent to himself.

-Well, I'm headed back uptown. Can I give anyone a lift?

-Thank you, Lieutenant, but Susan and I have our own transport. Irene? Would you like to stop off at your place and pick up a few things?

-Yes. That would be wonderful.

-Then, I suggest that we all head in our separate directions.

Susan shook her head in bemusement. Her mother had a knock of taking command of just about any situation.

Lt. Donovan stepped into the elevator and manned the controls. Marlena, Susan and Irene followed him in.

-Mendez? You coming?

-Not just yet. Thanks.

Edward waved goodbye and walked toward his father's office at the end of the narrow corridor. He didn't bother to knock. He just walked in and sat down.

-I've been expecting you, Edward.

-I know. And, I want you to level with me...about everything.

-That's a pretty broad expectation.

-I've got plenty of time...now. We all have, right?

-Yes. But, we need to check a few dates.

-But, the big details of life and death are settled?

It was both a question and a statement.

-Yes. Most definitely. I felt the "shift" of the planet upon its own grid line: the sun never disappeared, the asteroid was never a threat to the Earth or the moon. Rest easy on that score.

Edward was swept with a wave of relief.

-Good. I will. But, it's some of the little scores that concern me.

Manuel Mendez leaned back and smiled broadly at his son.

-Don't worry. You've an iron clad alibi for Miss Lisa Pabst's murder.

-Was I a suspect?

-Only for the briefest of times. But, Yolanda and a Sgt. Rayno vouched for your whereabouts at the time of that woman's murder.

Edward took out a cigarette and lit up.

-Pays to have friends.

-Edward, forget the past and focus on the present and the future.

The P. I. exhaled some cigarette smoke toward the ceiling.

-Like "normal," everyday people?

-Lorraine Keyes, for instance. A murder case that's right up your alley. I think it might prove to have many "layers" to it.

-How do you know about Lorraine Keyes?

-I listen to the news broadcasts: local as well as world events interest me. And, I have a feeling about that particular case.

-Hos so?

-Difficult to pinpoint. Why not get to work on it?

-I don't work gratis.

Manuel Mendez reached into the top right hand desk drawer. He withdrew a packet of money.

-Here's your retainer fee: $10,000.

He handed the money over to Edward who took it and counted it.

-That's quite a retainer fee. And, why so much? And, where did you get this much money from, if you don't mind my asking?

-You've earned it by saving this world once again. Here.

Manuel Mendez reached into the same top drawer.

-And, another $10,000 for services rendered. No arguments. Take it, shamus.

He threw this wad of money on to the desk.

-And, as to how I "got" it? Don't be so damned impertinent, young man. I don't explain myself to anyone. Now, leave me. I've much to think about.

-Just one question: does the sun have anything to do with time travel? Couldn't help but notice that the crack of dawn was a "key" factor in our round trip through time.

-Very good. Yes. The sun and the inclination of the Earth's axis...all play an essential part...a part that even I don't fully understand.

Manuel Mendez heaved a sigh.

-Please, Edward, I am exhausted, rather. I was up most of the night.

-I understand.

Edward picked up the second wad of money from the desk. He put out his cigarette and left the room. He walked down the narrow corridor to the elevator and was about to press the "down" button when an office door opened just to his right.

-Edward?

-Jamie! Oh, man. I didn't think you'd be here.

-Of course I'm here. But, somehow, I had the feeling that I was waiting with a group of people who I just met. But, they're gone...I think. I'm really not too sure what I'm trying to say. I'm a little confused and I don't know why.

-Jamie...I asked you to meet me here and you did.

-That, I remember. And, you gave me something to hold for you. Here, Edward. It's your pack of Lucky Strike.

-Thanks for keeping it. Have you been waiting long?

-No. Not at all. You went up to the roof only a few minutes ago.

-Let's head on down and...have I got a story to tell you.

-As long as you're back...that's all I care about. For some reason, I thought that I'd never see you, again.

Edward smiled and put his arm around Jamie's waist.

-You're gonna' be seeing a lot of me, baby.

Lt. Donovan got back to his office at the 86th Precinct House. He sat down at his desk not quite knowing what to do first. At the moment, he just wanted to catch his breath and breathe a sight of earned relief. Actually, he wanted to put his feet up on his desk.

He decided to order out for coffee. He picked up the phone and dialed down to the corner delicatessen for two containers of coffee. He put the receiver back down and waited for the two coffees to be delivered. And, he thought about Alexandra Raymond. He missed her. He missed her so much that he was about to page her when someone knocked on his office door.

-Come in.

It was Alexandra Raymond.

-Lieutenant? I have some notes that I'd like you to look at.

-You're just the person I wanted to see. Come on in and sit down. I've ordered up some coffees for us. Hope you don't mind.

Alex Raymond sat down.

-I'd love a cup.

Lt. Donovan smiled at the pretty young woman sitting opposite him.

-Alex, I missed you. I was on an assignment and I kept hoping that you had been there with me.

-Why Lt. Bill Donovan, you flatterer, you.

-It's the truth, Alex. You're a good woman to have by a man's side...my side.

-Bill, thank you so much for saying that.

-Are you free tonight? I'd like to take you to dinner.

-You can pick me up at seven.

Alex stood up and walked around to the Lieutenant's side of the desk. She bent over and kissed him.

-It'll be our first date.

-Edward?

-Yes, Marlena?

-I seem to have this vague recollection of being in possession of several books...unusual books that dealt with science and politics.

-You can't find them, can you?

-No. And, I've made a thorough search. Susan has that same vague recollection.

Edward explained the erasure of events in past time...but how the subconscious holds on to them.

-Fascinating. Truly.

Edward finished his whiskey and soda. It was early in the morning to have a drink, but what the hell? He dropped off Jamie at her job on his way uptown.

-Where's Irene and Susan?

-Irene is going over those notes that you took from Lisa Pabst. She seems quite interested in them. Susan is helping her. Here. Let me freshen your drink.

-Thanks. So, Marlena, what have you been up to?

-Oh...this n' that.

-Don't you trust me?

-Of course, dear boy. Here's your drink.

-Thanks.

-I'll be more specific. There's an exhibit at the Museum of Natural History this fall of Sumerian artifacts. I've procured an invitation to a private showing. Would you care to come along with us?

-"Us?"

-With Susan and Miss Wong, if she can manage it.

-I'd like that. And, didn't that girl, Valerie Spender, have an amulet that was a Sumerian artifact?

Marlena smiled approvingly at her friend.

-She did. And, I still have it. Your memory for details is excellent...as good as my own.

-Who gave Miss Spender that amulet?

-I've no idea and neither did her sister. I'm certain of that.

Edward took another sip of his drink.

-Any idea what's in this particular collection?

-An urn...the urn that was once sacred to the god Enki.

-A Sumerian god, I take it?

-You could call him that.

-What would *you* call him, Marlena?

-An alien...an alien from the forgotten planet.

-An alien?

-Yes. Or an ancestor of mankind, if you would. Do you think you'll be free to come? I'd value your impressions, Edward.

-I might. I've got a murder to investigate so I might be kind of busy. Don't know just how long that will take.

-Lorraine Keyes? Yes. I've read about her in the papers. You must keep me updated on it. Not just your run-of-the-mill murder, I'm assuming.

-Bull's eye.

It was a murder investigation that would take much longer than the P. I. could imagine.

Next

THE STRANGE CASE OF LORRAINE KEYES

An Edward Mendez, P. I. Thriller
Book X

About the Author

Gerard Denza has worked in the Publicity Dept. of Random House and Little, Brown and Company in New York City. He's worked with such authors as Pete Hamill, Willie Morris, Pat Booth and Arthur C. Clarke.

He is also the playwright and director of several Off-Off Broadway plays:

Icarus

Mahler: The Man Who Was Never Born

The Dying God: A Vampire's Tale

Shadows Behind the Footlights

The Housedress

His noir play, **Edmund: The Likely**, has been recorded for radio broadcast.

Mr. Denza is a graduate of Fordham University where he majored in Psychology and graduated Magna Cum Laude. He is hard at work on his next **Edward Mendez, P. I. Thriller** novel.